The River Bank

The River Bank

A sequel to Kenneth Grahame's
The Wind in the Willows

by

Kij Johnson

Endpaper, chapter, and incidental illustrations

by

Kathleen Jennings

Small Beer Press
Easthampton, MA

Small Beer Press
150 Pleasant Street #306
Easthampton, MA 01027
smallbeerpress.com
weightlessbooks.com
info@smallbeerpress.com

Distributed to the trade by Consortium.

Library of Congress Cataloging-in-Publication Data

Names: Johnson, Kij, author. | Jennings, Kathleen (Illustrator), illustrator.
Title: The river bank : a sequel to Kenneth Grahame's The wind in the willows
  / by Kij Johnson ; endpaper, chapter, and incidental illustrations
  throughout by Kathleen Jennings.
Description: First edition. | Easthampton, MA : Small Beer Press, [2017]
Identifiers: LCCN 2016059749 (print) | LCCN 2017007433 (ebook) | ISBN
  9781618731302 (hardback : alk. paper) | ISBN 9781618731319
Subjects: LCSH: Toad of Toad Hall (Fictitious character)--Fiction. |
  Animals--Fiction. | Friendship--Fiction. | Country life--England--Fiction.
  | River life--England--Fiction. | BISAC: FICTION / Literary. | FICTION /
  Classics. | FICTION / Fairy Tales, Folk Tales, Legends & Mythology. |
  FICTION / Historical. | GSAFD: Fantasy fiction.
Classification: LCC PS3560.O379716 R58 2017 (print) | LCC PS3560.O379716
  (ebook) | DDC 813/.54--dc23
LC record available at https://lccn.loc.gov/2016059749

First edition 1 2 3 4 5 6 7 8 9

Text set in Adobe Caslon Pro. Titles set in Didot.

Printed on 50# 30% PCR recycled Natures Natural paper by the Maple Press in York, PA.

Contents

For Elizabeth Bourne—my Lottie, my Beryl;
and for Barbara Webb, who is in at all the kills.

"Good friends, good books, and a sleepy conscience:
this is the ideal life."
—Mark Twain

Chapter One
New Arrivals

The news was everywhere on the River Bank and had been heard as far as the Wild Wood: Sunflower Cottage just above the weir had been taken by two female animals, and it was being set up for quite an extended stay. More, it was all being done *properly*, the River Bank's housewives all agreed. There was none of this casual, slapdash housekeeping that bachelor gentlemen were so apt to consider sufficient.

Every rag and stick of the cottage's contents had been turned out into the bright June daylight—and this was a surprisingly glorious June, with long days of bright golden sunlight, the countryside glowingly green from the rain which fell, in the most mannerly way, only at night—and everything scrubbed until it shone. The housewives all especially approved of this part of the activity because it gave them a good look at the cottage's furnishings. It had belonged for many years to an aged bachelor Hare, who had kept no housekeeper and only a single Rabbit who "did" for him; and indeed, it was all very satisfying, just dirty enough to vindicate them in their general disparagement of bachelors, without lessening to any degree their affection for the old Hare, now passed on to his reward.

The roof had been mended, and a moderately trustworthy Stoat hired and set to weeding the flower beds and rolling out the little lawn until it was smooth as a tennis court.

A spanking-new covered stove had arrived from Town and been installed. A travelling sweep had spent a highly productive afternoon with brushes and rods. Whitewash had been splashed about with liberality. Curtains had been washed, pressed, and rehung. A new water barrel had been purchased and painted bright blue.

And then there had arrived cartloads and cartloads of furnishings and supplies: jams and hams and cheeses and candles; bedding; a immense vase wrapped in burlap and filled with mixed peacock feathers and umbrellas; a number of heavy-framed pictures wrapped in flannel; a battered writing-desk; two glorious, shining bicycles with little wicker baskets; a sewing machine with an iron treadle; and boxes, crates, satchels, trunks, and undifferentiated parcels of every shape and size. The housewives nodded their approval. This was doing a thing right.

And last and best, in a dogcart up from the station on the first really hot day of the summer, the new arrivals themselves: a young Mole lady—everyone knew her proper name was Beryl, though no one could say just how they had discovered this—and her dear friend, the Rabbit. Several members of the neighborhood had contrived to be present when they first appeared. An old Mouse bent nearly double had chanced to be resting on the stile at the bottom of the cottage's garden, and said later that they looked to be very proper young animals. Beryl was wearing a travelling-dress as neat as it was pretty, in a glossy dark-brown silk trimmed with velvet bands, and a cap surmounted with a little velvet bow.

"The Rabbit, though," said the old Mouse. "She looks a bit silly, with all those silk cherries on her hat, and them pink ribbons! But aren't they all," the Mouse added. "Rabbits is always right flighty."

The satisfaction felt by the feminine residents of the River Bank was not, alas, universal. A few days after the arrival of Beryl and the Rabbit, the Mole said to his friend, the Water Rat, "I do not see what all this fuss is about. We were going along very well without these two setting everything at sixes and sevens."

Even the Rat, a confirmed bachelor, felt this was unjust. "Now, Mole, that's not fair; you know it's not. There was a lot of *here*-ing and *there*-ing at first, but now things are nearly as they were. The young ladies keep to themselves. Why, we hardly see them!"

The Mole and the Water Rat had been on the River since early that morning, a day that had dawned full of charming promise. In the matter of a single short hour, an expedition was called for, funded, provisioned, manned, and launched, and the two had set off with the Water Rat's boat packed to the gunwales with baskets, cushions, and fishing tackle. It had been a productive day in regards to fish-catching, luncheon-eating, pipe-smoking, and nap-taking; and now, as the sun lowered itself towards the distant trees, and the gnats rose from the cooling, gurgling, chuckling waters of the River, and the swifts dashed among them, the two friends were returning to the Water Rat's snug hole in the Bank: the Mole pleased to exercise his growing skills with the oars, the Rat content to let him do the work and with rare tact refraining from correcting his form.

They were passing Sunflower Cottage. The new inhabitants were not themselves visible, but a steady plume of smoke rose from the kitchen chimney, and there came on the cooling breeze the distinct scent of something or other baking. Windows were open, and flowers in pitchers were bright on every sill: a sight that ought to have brought joy to any beholder; except that it did not, apparently, to the Mole.

"Keeping to themselves means they're up to something," said the Mole grimly. "Females nearly always are."

The Water Rat chided, "Moley, is that fair? Is that just?"

"Yes," said the Mole baldly. "That is *exactly* what they are like."

The Rat leaned back and eyed the cottage, falling behind them now. "I should have thought you might like to have another Mole around. It makes things more homey, I should have said."

The Mole made a noise that sounded like "Pfaugh," or its equivalent, and added, forgetting his grammar, "'Homey' is exactly what I do *not* want. No, Ratty, I do see what you mean, and I am sure they are very nice animals, but—females, you know. You *know* what they are like! All musical soirees, and visits to Town for tooth-drawings, and endless washings-up, and clean collars, and morning visits and flower-pressing expeditions and tussie-mussies and—"

"Watch out!" the Water Rat cried; the Mole, by now quite het up, was rowing so hard and with so little attention that he stood a real risk of driving the boat its full length onto the bank, which just here came down as a grassy, reedy slope to the water's very edge. The Mole caught himself and, quite shamefaced, reversed oars.

"I *am* sorry, Ratty! I did not mean to become so . . ." He trailed off. "I must have become a sad bore. I do apologize."

"I understand," the Rat said kindly. "I really do, Moley. Everything was going on so well before this, and now you see everything disrupted."

"Precisely!" exclaimed the poor Mole. "I don't see why we need anyone else. We went along admirably without them."

The Water Rat laughed. "If we on the River Bank had said that a few years back, we should have hustled you right back to your snug cave, and *I* should be out a good friend, and *you* would never have learned about boating. Moley, how can you crab so? I think it is only because one of the new residents is a Mole lady."

"That is not it at all," said the Mole, a little crossly. "In fact—" But he cut himself off abruptly, and when the Water Rat looked at him in surprise, he said no more, only shook his head, a stubborn, secretive expression on his normally open face.

The wise Rat cocked an eye at the Mole. "Well, as to that," he said at last, peaceably, "if it's fancy teas and croquet on the lawn they'll be wanting, I am sure Toad does that better than we ever shall. No, they shall keep to their own doings, I expect—cooking, or needlepoint, or whatever it is that females do with their days. For myself— O, I *say*, Moley," he went on in quite a different tone, "there's the Badger! I haven't seen him in days, I don't think. Ahoy, Badger!" This last in a cheery, open-throated shout.

The Badger had been walking with some force along the path beside the River; but at the hail he looked up and saw them, and made as though to come down the bank directly, with such clear intent that the Water Rat directed the Mole to pull close beneath a low-hanging willow just ahead. The Mole managed this without assistance, looping the painter over a low branch as though born to the water: so competently, indeed, that the Rat said, "Well done, Mole!" as he leapt across to the verge. The Mole felt his heart swell with pride.

"Out raking?" said the Badger.

The Rat replied pleasantly, "A perfect day for an outing, we thought—and we did well, in the way of trout. I would have imagined you'd be in the Wild Wood this fine day, regulating Stoats, or monitoring Weasels, or some such."

The Badger shook his great shaggy head, and in his rough, low voice said, "No, all is well—or as well as it can ever be, with Stoats. They will break out into some wretched excess again, I am sure, but there has been none of *that* lately." *That* was referring to the events of the past winter, when quite a number of the less trustworthy animals had forgotten their place entirely and invaded the stately mansion, Toad Hall, ruining the furnishings and drinking up all the port, and in general validating everyone's low opinion of them.

"Where are *you* off to, Badger?" said the Mole.

"I am on my way to Toad's," said the Badger. "I want to have a quick word with him before he sits down to dinner."

"I hope he is not doing anything foolish again," the Rat said, a little severely. "We have all had quite enough of *that* from him." This time, *that* was referring to Toad's recent passion for motor-cars, the latest (and, as they all hoped but rather doubted, last) disastrous enthusiasm in a life rather overfull of disastrous enthusiasms; and incidentally a contributing factor in the Stoats' and Weasels' recent misbehaviors.

"No," said the Badger soberly. "I think he has learnt his lesson at last, and is committed to being a higher, better Toad. He has been interesting himself in the estates, just as his father would like to see. It is true that he has only managed to sell the Low Pasture to three different people without meaning to; and he has purchased a corn-thresher that he does not need; and it is true that he has also hired (at immense expense) an architect to draw up plans for a tourist-camp to be built upon the South Lawn; but you must admit that he is trying."

"Very trying!" laughed the Water Rat. "Well, I am sure he shall ask you to dine with him, and Toad is the very best of good hosts; but come sup with us, instead. It won't be but a bite, but Mole here proved most amazingly effective as a trout-catcher; and trout has to be eaten up fresh or there's no good in it."

"I will," assented the Badger. "I am recalling to his mind an obligation he has, as the master of Toad Hall, and he may not relish the intrusion, so I shall be very happy to say my piece and leave."

"Well, you can tell us all about it when you come back for supper. If we're still awake!" the Rat said, with another laugh.

They were indeed still awake when the Badger came at last down the little graveled path to the Water Rat's front door. It had taken longer to unload the boat than it had to load it, as they were quite tired and a bit stupid with fatigue, so that everything had required about twice as long as it should have; and when the Rat had decided a pipe and a "bit of something" (in this case, foaming, cool ginger beer drawn from a very attractive little barrel in his cellar, served in pewter tankards) was absolutely required before they settled down to the toil of preparing the fish, the Mole had not disagreed but only said, "Yes, rather," and then, a short while later, "Perhaps another?"

It was nearly full dark when the Badger at last appeared. He met the Mole bringing up the fish from the water's edge, cleaned now and stacked nose-to-tail in an old wooden trencher. They walked in together to find the revitalized Rat bent over a spitting-hot frying pan. "Cold fried potatoes, fried eggs, pickled onions, rocket and tomatoes, and bread, of course, and a custard and a bit of plum cake after, is all," said that noble animal briefly. "And the trout, of course. Just a snack, really; I feel almost bad about keeping you from Toad's board. How did he take your visit?"

The Badger opened his mouth to speak, but the Mole shook his head decidedly. "*No*, Ratty. Badger will start talking and you will start asking questions and forget to watch the fish, and we shall end up with all news and no supper. No. Supper and *then* news."

They ate on the Water Rat's little lawn, and it was as splendid as the best of such late-night picnic meals can be, jolly and casual and just a bit messy. And gossipy: when the food had all been eaten and the Badger and the Water Rat had lit their pipes, there was all sorts of news to share, for everyone was busy along the River Bank, as well as in the Wild Wood. "And the Wide World, for all we know," said the Badger. "It is June there, too. Their senses cannot be so dead that they do not heed it."

"So, Badger, what do you think of our new neighbors?" said the Water Rat presently.

"O, Ratty, no," moaned the Mole; but the Badger seemed not to hear.

"I have not met them yet," he said, "but they are said to be perfectly pleasant animals. The young Mole lady—"

"Beryl," said the Mole, in a low, dejected tone.

"—keeps very much to herself, I understand: a very proper, dignified young animal. They say she spends all her mornings inside, doing no one knows what. As for Miss Rabbit . . ." He knocked the ashes from his pipe onto the table. Delightful life! To dine at night out of doors, and knock out one's pipe just so, and cast one's crumbs to the wind, and pour the dregs of ginger beer grown warm into the grass; and all the cleaning-up left for morning. "Well," continued the Badger, "Rabbits are irresponsible, but she seems no worse than the rest of them, and better than some. At least our new neighbors seem free of many of the flitterings-about to which so many young females are inclined."

"I do not see—" muttered the Mole, but the Badger only continued.

"And *that* is what I have been about tonight. I reminded our friend of his duties as Toad of Toad Hall, and recommended he invite them to tea the day after tomorrow—"

"Badger, why—" exclaimed the Mole, more loudly this time.

"—on the terrace, weather permitting." The Badger cast a knowledgeable eye on the glowing night sky, which was cloudless and filled with stars, for the moon had not yet risen. "But I think this weather should hold, until then at least. I suggested champagne punch, as a proper light beverage for ladies," he ended.

"Badger, no!" the Mole cried in what was very nearly a shout, loud enough that a Duck sleeping down the bank a bit called out, "Steady, guv'nor! Can't a body get his forty outside and get the good of the fresh air without a lot of bellerin' and hollerin' in the wee hours?"

The Mole apologized and continued in a lower tone. "How could you bring this up with Toad? They will ruin everything."

The Badger's expression was hidden by the darkness, but he sounded disapproving. "It is Toad's duty, Mole. His is the great house in these parts, and it is up to Toad to make the young ladies officially welcome to the River Bank. Surely you would not like to see him be remiss in his duties, and thus besmirch the estimable name of Toad!"

"Well—" began the Mole, sounding as though that would not in fact bother him much, but the Badger interrupted.

"Mole, I am surprised at you. You, a Mole! Hitherto invariably courteous and gentlemanly; a generous host; a true and amiable friend. And yet, every time anyone mentions these young ladies, you become sullen and petulant—yes, I said 'petulant,'" the Badger said, as the Mole opened his mouth to object, "and I meant 'petulant.' Where is the *parfit gentil* Mole I have learned to hold up to others as a model of proper behavior?"

The Mole sighed. "Of course you are right. It's just—no. No," he said, more firmly. "You *are* right. A Mole does not shirk. I apologize to you, Badger—and you, Ratty. I am sure I have been a sad trial. They will disrupt everything in some uncomfortable fashion, I am sure; but that is no reason to be unpleasant about it all. I will do better."

"That is the Mole we admire," said the Badger approvingly. "When you come to Toad's tea, you shall see they are not so bad."

"Wait!" said the Mole. "You didn't say *we* had to meet them, as well!"

The Rat said lazily, "Don't be an ass, Moley, of course we're invited. It's *Toad*. He'll want moral support. And the food will be excellent, so there's that."

Chapter Two
Tea at Toad Hall

The weather remained fine for the Toad's tea party, and so it was that the Mole, the Water Rat, their friend the Otter, and the Badger were all standing together on Toad Hall's southern terrace wearing clean collars, everyone with his fur brushed until it glowed. Even the Badger had left behind his comfortable tweed hacking jacket, with the patches on the elbows and its sagging pockets full of pipe supplies and pen-knives and other interesting objects, and had donned instead an ancient, beautifully cut, but somewhat worn morning coat and trousers. He was turning the tall hat around in his paws by the brim, exchanging pleasantries with their host, the Toad.

"Waiting for females; typical," the Mole groused to the Rat—but softly, so that the others might not overhear. He scuffed a paw across the golden flagstones. "This is *precisely* the sort of disruption I meant: tight collars and every button buttoned and all that—when we could be halfway to the pike pond, just messing about; or getting out the things for lawn-bowling; or most anything but this."

But the Rat only chuckled and shook his head. "Just wait until the eating starts, and you will forgive everything." A few yards away, there were several small tables set with the snowiest linen, and an immense sideboard (brought out from the dining room so that the staff could hand things around in the most expeditious fashion) crowded intriguingly with trays, plates, salvers, cake-stands, pitchers, and jugs, all covered with lace-edged napkins. He went on, "No, I shouldn't mind being back into my old flannel bags, but this isn't so bad!"

"So long as that's *all* it is," began the Mole in a low voice. "You know Toad, Ratty. I shouldn't be surprised if he proved as susceptible to the attractions of young ladies as he is to motor-cars, caravans, and the like. It starts with tea but it could end anywhere at all, and I wouldn't dress up and stand around like this more than once, not for all the tea and cakes in the world."

But the Toad caught his last words and only said with a laugh, "O, Mole, don't be such a grouch! You look very dapper indeed. You all do; and it's worth everything just to see old Badger here in his finery. Very swank! Anyway, we are much too rustic here on the River Bank, *I* always say. We could all use some town-bronze. Well, nearly all of us." The Toad ran a paw lovingly down his lapel. He was quite glorious, shining in the sunlight in a white jacket of shockingly modern cut: short where it should be long, and narrow where it should be broad. It could not be said to flatter his figure, which was rather round than otherwise, but it was incontestably *le dernier cri*— or it might be, anyway; none of the other animals had ever seen anything like it before.

The Badger shook his head. "Toad, it is one thing for you to dress like this. You are rich and a known eccentric"—the Toad puffed up a bit at this, taking it for a compliment— "though what your father would have said about such a coat, I shall not speculate. But for you to encourage decent, proper fellows like the Mole here to imitate such a mode—"

"They're here!" the Otter exclaimed suddenly in a low voice, and the animals all turned. Indeed they were. Beryl and the Rabbit were being led around the corner of the house;

Beryl behaving very properly, her attention directed towards her host and expressing no more than the appropriate amount of pleasant anticipation; but the Rabbit staring all about her, her eyes enormous in her pretty, round face, and her ears twitching every which way. As they approached, she leaned close to whisper something into Beryl's ear while she gestured with one paw to the lawn leading down to the water's edge, a lawn large enough for any number of croquet games.

The Toad swelled visibly and was heard by the Mole to murmur to himself, "Quite, quite overcome, poor thing"; and then, in a louder voice, "Ladies, dear, *dear* ladies! You honor me! Welcome to my humble little patch of earth!" He approached and bowed, seizing and kissing Beryl's paw with great élan and an expression so self-congratulatory and complacent that the Badger made an untranslatable noise in his throat, and the Otter was taken with a sudden fit of coughing—presumably a gnat had flown into his mouth—and had to turn away for a moment.

The Water Rat and the Mole exchanged looks.

"O, dear," whispered the Water Rat. "It's going to be like *that*, is it?"

The situation was, in fact, not *quite* what they had feared—Toad's conceit would never permit him to fall in love at first sight (or any other sight) with any person but himself—but nevertheless, in all the ways that mattered, it was *exactly* like that.

"Dear ladies," again said the Toad, again bowing. "You are indeed welcome! We were just chatting, my friends and I, about how we chaps have grown far too casual here in the neighborhood, with no young ladies to incite, or inspire rather, those small acts of courtesy that have such a civilizing influence here in the country, that we, ah . . ." But he had lost himself in his sentence, and trailed off to a halt, looking a little silly.

"O, too kind!" interpolated the Rabbit in suffocated tones, but Beryl only nodded and said, very properly, "It was kind of you to invite us. Thank you so much." Her voice was low and calm, but was there perhaps a gleam of amusement in it? She surely wasn't laughing at *them*! The Mole, watching her pretty closely, could not be sure but had his suspicions.

"O, but you do not know my friends!" the Toad exclaimed pompously. "Allow me to introduce the Badger to you . . . a very respected member of one of our older families. . . . The Water Rat, a very pleasant chap. . . . The Otter, quite the gentleman. . . . *And,*" he said with great smugness, just as though he were selecting the correct ace from a deck of cards as part of a magic trick, "my dear, *dear* friend, the Mole!—Miss Mole and Miss Rabbit," he said to them all.

"How do you do," said everyone except the Mole, who mumbled something or other. Beryl added, with what might have been a deepening of the glimmer of a smile (if anyone had been certain whether she were smiling in the first place), "Mr Mole and I have met before this, though perhaps he does not recollect the occasion."

"You have?" exclaimed several voices at once, and various faces turned towards the Mole, but before anyone could inquire further, Beryl turned to the Toad and said, "What a charming place this is! You must tell us all about it."

And that was the end of that topic, for the moment, at least. Toad never needed much of an excuse to boast, and this was too fertile an opportunity to miss: two strangers who very likely could be counted upon not to interrupt him with the sorts of statements his friends were too apt to make—things like, "Don't be an ass, Toad," and, "Do stop *bragging*, old chap!" and, "What your father would say, I *don't* know."

The subsequent tour of the house and grounds was exhaustive. Seconded good-naturedly by the Otter, the Toad boasted his way through all the major rooms and offices, his words punctuated by *ooh*s and *o my!*s from the Rabbit, and, less satisfyingly, by Beryl's more restrained (but also more rational) compliments on such unexceptionable topics as the elegant proportions of the rooms.

The Rabbit was especially entranced by the Green Room, designed by the Toad's grand-father as a sitting room to set off his new wife's complexion— "So *romantic!*" she moaned. "Just like a *fairy* tale! The prince wins his bride!"

"Rabbit . . .," said Beryl in a tone that suggested to the suspicious Mole the rolling of eyes, but the Toad heard nothing of this and explained that it had just been restored at immense expense (he was prepared to tell them precisely how much, but was headed off from this by the Badger) after a pack of low Weasels and Stoats had destroyed it.

He added, "If you are interested at all in our little fraças last year, you may find the next room of even greater interest," and threw open a pair of doors.

It was a large room, an impressive room—what was called the Library and had actually been used as such by the Toad's father and grandfather before him—but now it had been turned into a sort of museum. The books had been shoved into the less-visible nooks and corners of the room, and the most prominent shelves were crowded with bits of rubble labeled things like: A PIECE OF THE CANOPY, FROM THE QUEEN-ANNE BEDROOM, EXCAVATED BY THE TOAD, and: UNIDENTIFIED SHERD, FROM THE BUTLER'S PANTRY, FOUND BY THE TOAD. There were as well weapons of every size and sort: swords, daggers, cutlasses, cudgels, staffs, and sticks. Over the mantel, the Toad had caused to be mounted a tasteful arrangement of crossed swords and pistols, clustered appetizingly on either side of a large painting in a gilded rococo frame, of a mighty Toad brandishing pistols in each hand, vanquishing quite a crowd of Weasels, Stoats, and Foxes, as a rather smaller Badger, Mole, and Water Rat looked on admiringly from the corners of the picture. There was some sort of a thunderstorm going on in the background, and a bit of sunlight breaking through managed to illuminate the Toad while leaving everything else in gloom. A small brass plate affixed to the frame read, *THE VALIANT TOAD, AMIDST THE FRAY.*

"What!" said the Badger, turning suddenly upon the hapless Toad. "What is this—this atrocity?"

"O, well, as to that," said the Toad with a careless gesture towards the mantel; "I thought you might not have seen this yet. I have only just finished putting the room back together. I had someone down from Town throw it together, a very up-and-coming young man, pictures in the Academy Exhibition and all that. I think he captured your dignity, your real *nobility* of expression, don't you?" he added, in a weaker voice. Toad had been rather dreading this disclosure and had hoped that the presence of such strangers as Miss Mole and the Rabbit—females, too—might mitigate to some degree the Badger's anticipated reaction: unsuccessfully, as it was turning out.

"Toad," said the Water Rat sternly, "this is appalling. What happened to the better, more modest Toad who made so many promises to us all last year? The Toad who would not aggrandize himself; the contrite Toad, who freely acknowledged his faults and strove to amend his behavior?"

The Toad said with a surprised expression, "Was I supposed to *remain* that way?"

Said the Badger, severely, "And it is worse than that. Toad, it is one thing for you to act foolish to *us*—we may be disappointed, but we are not at least surprised—but you have been lying to an *artist!* 'The Valiant Toad'—faugh! I only hope you paid him well for this . . . this *debasement* of his craft—" He held up his paw as the Toad opened his mouth. "No. I do not wish to know *how* well you paid. This all must be removed immediately, and the room returned to what it was."

"Quite right," nodded the Water Rat. "Really, Toad, what were you thinking?"

But the Rabbit exclaimed, "O, no! Mr Badger, do not say so! Such an exciting event, and everyone so courageous! It *should* be memorialized!" She pressed her paws together. "I am agog! Why, you are all heroes!"

"Well, as to that," the Toad said modestly but with one wary eye on the Badger. "I did not do so very much. It was these three that saved the day, you know. But I did do quite a lot of fighting, yes," he continued, perking up. "Quite mowed them down, you might say. Perhaps the ladies would like to repair to the tea tables? I am sure the lemonade shall be getting warm."

The lemonade was not warm, a tribute to the Toad's competent household staff, and they all fell to with a will. Toad Hall had always been famed for the excellence of its kitchens, bakery, and cellar, and in this at least the Toad had proved himself the equal of his father, and even of his grandfather, who had been famed throughout the county for his hospitality. There was Indian tea and Ceylonese tea and Chinese tea. There was lemonade and raspberry juice and champagne and claret and beer (the last for the Water Rat, but served in a goblet so as not to seem low). There were charming little sandwiches, some filled with watercress and others filled with pink shavings of ham, and yet others with a delicious orange paste that tasted of curry and chicken, and scones and cakes and—well, there was a lot of it, and it was all very good, and that is all I can say about *that* without going on for pages and pages and leaving you very dissatisfied with your own teas.

At his small table Toad had seated the young ladies to either hand, and the easygoing Otter with them. The Mole, the Rat, and the Badger were at a second table close beside the first; and thus separated from his most usual critics, the Water Rat and the Badger, the Toad absolutely let himself go.

"Well, it was no great matter," began the Toad in a self-effacing tone when the Rabbit asked him to tell her more about the attack upon Toad Hall. He cocked one eye at the Badger to see whether he were listening, but that worthy beast was in close conversation with the Water Rat and the Mole and evidently paying no heed; and as for the Otter, he was gazing at the Toad with affectionate interest and no apparent intention of queering the game. "I was away from home for some time—on business, you know—and returned to find that in my absence the place had been overrun by Wild Wooders. So I organized my friends, armed everyone, and off we went! There were hundreds of them, and, O, it was a battle! Hours of combat! Weasels, tossed from the windows! Stoats, cast into the River! Ferrets, weltering in their own gore! And who was it that did all this? Only Toad! A slash to the left—a Fox falls, thanks to Toad! A blow to the right—down goes a Cat! Toad, again! A fierce Capybara, escaped from the zoo, joins the fray! What now? Toad saves us all! Here, a Badger finds himself cornered by a score of villainous Weasels: What to do, what to do? A Toad to the rescue! There, a Water Rat weeping—"

"Toad!" The Badger's thundering voice from the other table caused the Toad to drop his butter knife, which he had been brandishing in a manner that boded ill for the Rabbit's whiskers, for she was leaning forward as far as she could, her eyes shining. "What bragging lies are you telling?"

"Lies?" the Toad exclaimed, with an affronted expression. "Badger, I am only telling them a bit of the history of last year's events. I have not forgotten (though you may have) that I have learnt my lesson—though I may have gotten carried away a bit, just at the end," he admitted.

"No, Toad, it was all mere fabrication, beginning to end." The Badger leaned across to Beryl. "Toad was *not* away on business at all. In fact, he was—"

"No, no," said the Toad, weakly. "The ladies don't need—"

"—in prison," the Badger said firmly. "For motor-car stealing. Madam, if you are to stay here, it is best that you know what sort of people your neighbors are."

"Motor-cars," Beryl said, though she sounded more amused than distressed. "Dear me, that is very bad; but perhaps it will not be such a great issue for the Rabbit and myself, as we do not have a motor-car. More tea, Mr Mole?"

"*And* horse-stealing," said the Water Rat, adding his mite. "And impersonating a washerwoman, and defrauding the rails, and horse-stealing—or did I say that already?"

"You did," said Beryl.

"You did," affirmed the Mole. "And there was a second motor-car theft, was there not? I cannot keep track."

"O, how thrilling!" said the Rabbit, her ribbons fluttering with excitement. "It is all exactly like the ancient Greeks!"

"Ulysses?" Beryl said drily. "Very likely."

"O, *Beryl*." The Rabbit looked reproachfully at her companion.

"It was all just a misunderstanding," explained the Toad to the Rabbit, taking little heed of Beryl, as he knew no Greeks ancient or otherwise, except for owning a very old vase covered with any number of them, all inadequately clad. "All most unfortunate. And there was no harm done! I escaped, *with* no aid whatsoever—charmed the jailor's daughter—tricked a railroad engine-driver, oh ho!—fooled an old canal-woman, *and* stole her horse, *and* sold it to great advantage—sweet-talked a fine breakfast from a gypsy: quite one of my brethren of the road and a very good chap—"

"*Very* like Ulysses," Beryl said, more drily still. The Mole opened his mouth as though to say something, but shut it again abruptly.

The Toad continued, unheeding, "And stole *again* the very motorcar that had started the whole thing! Could anyone else have done this? No, only Toad! Toad, the—" He suddenly noticed every eye upon him: the Rabbit's, round with wonder, but the rest expressing skepticism, amusement, and annoyance compounded in various proportions. He ended, in a more rational tone, "Anyway, all's well that ends well, I always say; and here I am, an entirely reformed Toad."

"All was *not* well," interjected the Water Rat. "Except for the barristers you had to pay, and the Exchequer you sent the fines to. *They* ended up well enough," he said with a grin.

But the Rabbit did not care. This Toad—this courageous, gay, *glorious* Toad—seemed to her a sort of *beau ideal*, precisely the sort of fellow a young animal might esteem and even strive to emulate. She exclaimed, "You are so very resourceful!"

"Not at all, not at all," the Toad said. "You seem a Rabbit of intrepidity. I am sure you have had adventures of your own."

"O no, nothing to compare," the Rabbit said with envy. "I have only been in a hot-air balloon ascent, and there was the time I became involved in a bank robbery. But they were very nearly accidents." She sounded regretful.

"Dear Lottie," said Beryl warningly, in a tone most of those present recognized, having used it themselves many times with the Toad. "I am sure the gentlemen do not care about our doings." It was clear that, by her intonation of the word, "our," Beryl meant "your."

But the Toad patted the Rabbit's hand patronizingly. "You have not of course had the same opportunities as I. Perhaps another time, I will share with you a few of my adventures, when I travelled across England in a caravan."

The Water Rat said rudely, "You mean, crashing it in a ditch within a few miles of home." This was all quite wearing to an animal of sense.

"A caravan!" the Rabbit cried, unheeding. "Of all the things, the activity I wish most to try!"

"Indeed?" said the Toad. "It was the neatest thing! I quite loved my caravan. So compact! Everything in its place! The open road before one! Indeed, I thought it was the *only* thing, until I began motoring."

"Motoring!" the Rabbit gasped, and clasped her paws together. "So you did not merely *steal* a motor-car? Perhaps you even *owned* one?"

The Toad bowed, one eye on the glowering Badger, whose expression was darkening by the minute, rather like a summer cloud just before the first thunderclap that presages the deluge. "Before I became the quiet, mannerly animal you see before you, I was indeed a motorist—the fastest, most dangerous, *riskiest* motorist that ever was! Before I reformed, that is," he added hastily.

But even the Mole had at last had enough. The Badger was speechless because he could not select which of the many hot words upon the tip of his tongue he wished first to say; and the Otter, most reprehensibly, was struggling not to laugh. The Mole whispered to the gaping Water Rat, "Cannot anyone stop that Rabbit? Toad is bad enough *without* encouragement, but she is absolutely inciting him and you know where *that* will end."

"I do indeed." The Water Rat eyed the Toad, who was visibly expanding under the Rabbit's admiring eye. "It will end, as Toad's exploits always end, with a wreck of some sort, and then constables. No, you are right, we must stop this." And when a moment came in the Toad's perorations into which he could interject a word, he said more loudly, "Toady, perhaps the young ladies would like to see the lime alley before they leave?"

Chapter Three
Arcadia

Beryl awoke suddenly in her soft little bed. What was it that had pulled her from her dreams? She had it. A bird had begun singing just beyond her open window, a complex trill so sweet in tone, so gay and bright, that she had awakened smiling and could not stop. What was that bird? She did not know it.

There was no going back to sleep, not in a day that had started with that lovely, liquid sound. She tossed aside the red counterpane and padded across the creaking wooden floor, so cool under her bare paws, to pull aside the curtain and push open the casement.

O, the smell! Beryl leaned out, breathed and breathed again until she was dizzy with that intoxicating blend of dew-wet grass and eglantine, meadow-sweet, and lupins; cows a long way off; and under it all, the scent of the River itself, a warm summertime odor of mud like yeast-bread rising, and pleasure-boats, and fish in their home.

And, O, the birds! She could not work out where was the bird that was singing so beautifully, only that it was somewhere at the foot of the cottage lawn; but now it was being joined by others, one and two and then ten and twenty others, until the air was filled with trills and warblings, the morning greetings of a city of trees and bushes filled with merry-hearted and very talkative residents. She recognized the monotone boom of a bittern down among the rushes (but how did she know that?), and an owl's deep hoot as she floated home after her short night's business (for she was complaining to herself: all this waking-up chattering, when any right-thinking bird knew that it was time for sleep!); and a wren's quick pattering melody. But there were others—so many others!—she did not recognize, and always, always amid the chorus, the enchanting, unknown song.

The sky, which had started out nearly dark, only the faintest promise of light in the east, was blooming now, all the colors of a summer's worth of flowers: rose and lavender and lilac shading into cornflower and delphinium and loosestrife, and everything changing even as she tried to record it all in her mind's eye; for Dawn can never be caught in more than snatches, each glimpse promising more than can ever be captured.

The world beneath that glowing sky was dimmed, softened by a haze of mist that gentled every outline, but she could still picture it all. There was the cottage's lawn and the enormous chestnut tree at its foot; there, the golden-graveled footpath that followed the bank; there, the dark slender spires of the lupins and rushes in their serried ranks; and there, best of all, the River itself, smooth with summer, whispering softly to herself as she idled past with the unhurried grace of a queen. And past the water, the far bank and its little fields and meadows, the tidy hedgerows spangled with hawthorns and dog-roses that shone like tiny stars; and then, nearly to the horizon, the black tangle of woods, and beyond that— nothing, only the sky, brighter and brighter.

And, O, the Dawn! Now the first rose-red sliver of the rising sun slid above the land, and all the world began to take on its proper colors, green and brown and gold, and the sky became the color of sky, and the air the color of air, and it was only then, after the day was truly begun, that she realized that, at some point in all that glorious dawning, the strange and lovely song had ended.

There came on her such a sense of urgency to get out into the July morning that she could not stay still. It seemed as though there was not a moment to lose, already so many moments lost. There was work to do today, but how could she, after such a song? She splashed herself with cold water from the ewer on her bureau, and dressed quickly.

"Rabbit! Rabbit!" she called as she pattered down the hall and threw open the Rabbit's bedroom door. "Get up!" she said, and snatched a pillow away. "It is the most beautiful day!" But the Rabbit only gave a soft howl and pulled another pillow over her ears. Beryl, knowing the signs, gave her up for lost and ran down the stairs.

In a corner of the shady parlor, close beside a window, was her writing desk. A quire of creamy laid paper was stacked neatly in one corner; her green-celluloid fountain pen with its black cap and its gold fittings atop it; the ink-bottle beside another pile of pages covered with Beryl's tidy copperplate handwriting: The Novel.

Beryl was an Authoress. Her first novel had been secretly written on a little table in the room she shared with one of her sisters, and no one had been more surprised than she when she had sent it to a Publisher, and that Publisher had Published it. *The Haunted Treasure of Bone Island* had been bound in pale-blue buckram with a very exciting picture embossed in three colors upon the cover, of a sailing ship, pirates (one with a peg leg), a ghost, and a great conflagration; with the title in gold above it, and below it (also in gold) her name, B. P. Mole. There had been four novels since then: *The Counsel of Storm Rock*; *The Iron Hare of Chateau Sang*; *19 Croquet Lane*; and *M. Bourne, Vivisectionist*; and (except for *19 Croquet Lane*, which had posted disappointing sales; no one, it turned out, was much interested in a B. P. Mole novel without a single supernatural visitation), each had been more popular than the previous one.

The Novel! She had tentatively entitled it *Philotera's Horror*. There was a calm yet plucky heroine; a locked, battered iron box with a missing key and mysterious runes scratched across its lid (perhaps cursed; Beryl hadn't decided yet); a ruined estate in Cornwall (for research she was relying heavily upon a souvenir folder of tourist postcards entitled Scenic Cornwall, Land of Tintagel!); an ancient sage who existed in the novel solely to pass on to the heroine a forbidden secret of mind-control, and immediately afterward to die before her horrified eyes; a poisonous serpent being kept as a pet in a basket in the villain's lair (which Beryl knew would come in handy for the plot at some point); and an endangered orphanage filled with children that reminded the heroine of herself when she was a lass. Every morning from nine until lunchtime Beryl wrote, and from three in the afternoon until teatime she revised her work, writing it out again clean. She was on page two hundred and six.

Every morning—but not this divine morning, not when the air was intoxicating and filled with golden light and adventure. Spend the day in a stuffy parlor making a mess of perfectly good blank paper? Stringing drab words together without a hope of any spark to set them afire? Working out the really very dreary doings of her uninteresting heroine, some way to paste over the gaps in her (she saw it now) contrived and artificial plot? And all the while, just outside her window, the glowing green of the lawn, the lovely clouds in the sky, the first boating parties on the River; the River itself, its easy low laughter as it burbled? Rather not!

"I need a holiday, I think," she said aloud.

As she passed through the parlor, the Novel spoke to her as a housemate does when one first enters the breakfast room, looking up from the morning newspaper with a welcoming smile but saying no more than, "I say, have you heard—?" The Novel spoke pleasantly to Beryl, but she only shook her head impatiently, as though to say, *Not now; there is something more urgent on my mind*: a thing that, in that hypothetical breakfast room, would be coffee; but that, here and now, on this divine morning, was nothing less than the urgent call of the world itself.

With a flicker of guilt she filched a sheet of paper from the Novel's virgin quire, to scratch out a note to the Rabbit— but standing at the desk, so as not to get ensnared. The Novel whispered to her, coaxed her, hectored her, shouted at her, but she ignored all its pleas and demands. In the end, it let her go, as one finally opens the back door to let out a whining dog to run in circles for a few minutes before it is called back inside.

From the cool, dark larder Beryl collected half a loaf of bread, some butter in a rough little pottery tub, a corked bottle of fizzy lemonade, and a corkscrew—for she was a sensible Mole, the sort of person who liked to plan ahead and did not leave things to chance; not at all like her heroine, in fact. She tucked everything into a little knapsack along with a novel she was reading (for research purposes), entitled *The Corpse with the Missing Toe*, then she slipped out the door and down to the toolshed at the bottom of the lawn, where she kept her bicycle.

The River greeted her as though they were old friends who had made plans for this morning: a rippling, endless, affectionate chuckle, confidential and quiet, as though trying not to wake anyone else up and have them horn in on the fun: pleased with its company and the prospect of a day together. The rising sun flickered upon the River's dancing surface, sparking reflections on the toolshed wall and the undersides of the overhanging elms. Dragonflies as big as Beryl's paw hovered above the water. A heron appeared suddenly, its vast wings making an audible sound as it flew upstream, to some hidden hunting ground.

Beryl removed her bicycle from the toolshed, checked its tires and its brakes (she *was* a sensible Mole), and then she was off, pedaling along the river-path. The sun was still not quite clear of the horizon.

Mile after mile. The crunch of gravel beneath the bicycle wheels mingled with the endless chuckling sound of the River and the birdsong everywhere. The river-path passed a stand of poplars and then plunged into a shrubbery that went down to the water's edge itself.

She came to a place where a canal opened into the River, and she paused a moment at the top of the little bridge to remove her jacket and put it into the bicycle's wicker basket, for, early as it was, the day was growing hot. On one side, the canal was a calm band of dark water that threaded past reeds and rushes and water-meadows—could she see water lilies, in a half-hidden inlet?—losing itself under an arched stone bridge some distance away to the west. Just below the bridge it opened into the River. At first the River rejected the canal water, which remained a dark streak against its muddier brown, with coils and curls where the two waters greeted one another warily; but the River's brown triumphed at last. They combined and the canal's limpid darkness was lost; and on the augmented River went, on and on, joined by other canals and rivers and streams, on and on, until it came to the Sea and was in its turn vanquished.

Beryl was looking down into the water musingly and saw a coracle upon the river, an unfamiliar Mouse (but so many of the River Bank folk were still strangers to her) on her way to the morning's shopping, with her daughter plying the oars. "Nice weather, miss," the Mouse called up, with the closest she could get to a respectful curtsey without standing up in the coracle. Even so, it bobbed and wobbled in a way that made her daughter say, "Steady on, Mum!"

"Yes, lovely," said Beryl. Common courtesy demanded a pleasant reply (and in any case, it was too beautiful a day for anything less than the cheeriest of words), but before she could say more the coracle and its occupants were past, out of earshot and hidden by the rushes along the River Bank. But perhaps it was for the best that her trance had been broken, or she might have spent all that morning upon the footbridge.

Mile after mile rolled away beneath the wheels of her bicycle. She felt the changes in the path through the tires: here gravel, there a drying puddle, there earth beaten down iron-hard beneath a slick of sticky mud, across a lawn or field. The path ducked beneath a metalled road bridge. She reveled in the moment of cool, damp darkness, and the sounds overhead of horses pulling a heavy dray, and then a motor-car. "They have no idea I am down here," she said to herself. "Why, I might be a spy! Or a bandit, setting an ambush. If there were two of us, now. . . ." She thought of writing down a few details that might be useful for the Novel, but she had no paper nor a pen, and— "O, hang the book!" she said, for by then the bicycle had swept her back into the sunlight, which glanced down in patches through the trees. The stately pile of Toad

Hall was ahead of her upon the opposite bank—the gold stone and gothic arches, the many chimney pots, the gardener trimming a hedge—all so much more interesting and lovely than any words she could contrive.

Beyond Toad Hall she was in unfamiliar country, for she had never gone so far before this and had brought no map. The River was still her friend, still chuckling, but younger upstream, a little wilder, perhaps. Throughout the morning, she had passed River Bankers on the path, but the heat of the day had driven many of them home or onto the water,  and perhaps fewer of them lived up here. She passed blackberry brambles, the first black fruits ripening on their bushes, and realized that she was thirsty and very hungry. She stopped to collect handful of berries, rather staining her fingers and the linen handkerchief in which she collected them. They tasted warm and sweet and tart; but she ate only a few, for she did not want to spoil her luncheon.

She stopped again just a little farther on, when she came to a sheep-cropped field. Leaving her bicycle beside the path, she walked up to a lone oak upon the crest of a hill. She spread a cloth on the grass there, and there she laid out her picnic— the bread and sweet butter, the sun-heated blackberries, and the bottle of fizzy lemonade, quite warm now and not nearly as nice as she had imagined it would be early that morning, though still refreshing.

She looked about her as she ate. She could see far in nearly every direction: to the north-east, where the Town lay (though it was not visible, of course); south-east down to Toad Hall, and beyond it, a village with a church steeple and an inn and a parsonage and a few shops and some cottages: a village for men and women and their children; just to the south of that, the great bend of the River that was home. She stared and stared, but could see nothing of Sunflower Cottage's red-tiled roof. Was that the big chestnut, down by the water? The River glittered under the noonday sun. Just on the horizon to the south was the great dark tangle of the Wild Wood, where she knew the Badger lived, along with any number of uncivilized animals.

She did not rise from her comfortable position leaning against the tree to face west, for she knew already just what was behind her: more fields and copses and farmsteads and villages; streams and rivers and the canal, curving off to the north; and then, miles and miles away, to the north-east, the busy, busy Hills, where she and the Rabbit were from.

The Hills! It was a world as busy as the River Bank—in its own way, busier. The Hills were pasturage and fields, long smooth slopes of grass kept short by sheep and cattle, scattered with copses of beech and oak and ash, and long narrow strips of trees tucked into the folds between the hills. The spaces were more open, and people were not so common a sight, so the animals there—the *nice* animals: Moles, Rabbits, Hares, Hedgehogs, Mice, and all the rest, though to be sure the others, the Foxes and Voles and such, were common enough as well—were often out and about, doing their shopping, or calling upon one another, or joining little Improving Societies where one might learn drawn-threadwork or see magic-lantern shows about Africa. It was not always an easy life, but it was usually a jolly one.

The River Bank was less—*bumptious*, she supposed she must say. The residents did not rush about and shout across lanes quite so often; they did not run through the dew in nothing but their chemises for sheer simple joy on a lovely July morning. The young males of the River Bank did not dare one another to go down and tease the farm dogs. But she liked everyone she had met here. They were pleasant, entertaining, and willing to let her live her life just as she wished.

Though, what of the Mole? He had been quite rude every time she encountered him, and more than once she had seen him duck into a convenient copse of trees rather than meet her face-to-face. Whenever they had been jointly guests at Toad Hall, he had said almost nothing to her; though in any case, it was hard to get a word in edgewise with the Toad, and he could be forgiven for silence, if only it had not been accompanied by a brooding frown whenever he looked at her. Well, Moles were solitary fellows by nature—she was herself, she knew. Though the Rabbit was entertaining company, she became a little fatiguing from time to time. Why should the Mole feel any differently?

Laughing to herself, she picked up the *The Corpse with the Missing Toe* and in only a few moments was deeply immersed. The resolution of the macabre murder of a notable philanthropist was coming to a head, and she was agog to see how the author reconciled the suspicious (but possibly unrelated) behaviors of his brother, his widow, and his chauffeur.

She awoke suddenly some time later to hoarse breathing in her ear, and the overwhelming smell of chewed grass and wool. A sheep, wandering over to learn more of this foreign invader into its territory, had discovered the remains of the bread and begun snuffling over Beryl's clothing, looking for more. She leapt to her feet with something very like a shriek, and the startled sheep somersaulted head over heels and stared at her with enormous resentful eyes before bleating once, indignantly, and trotting back to its fellows.

She looked around her, brushing bits of masticated grass from her skirt. She had slept for perhaps an hour or a little more, but in that short while, everything had changed. The morning's delightful coolness was gone, even its memory faded to nothing under the unrelenting midafternoon sun. The heat cloaked everything in a white, ungentle haze. In the distance the River shone hot and hard as a sheet of steel. A line of ants led to the empty butter crock and another away, and a fly buzzed on the last of the blackberries. Beryl felt a little sweaty and quite head-achey, as one does when one naps outside on a hot day.

"O, bother," she said aloud. And then, "O, *bother*"—for the glorious day was lost, to her anyway. The Novel had grown tired of waiting for her to return from her holidaying and was summoning her now in the peremptory fashion of a dog-owner calling his animal back to heel. She still had no interest in the words, nor the characters nor the plot, nor the desk in the parlor, nor any part of the Novel; but that did not matter. The Novel had judged it was long enough, and had whispered into her ear, "Remember, thou art a writer."

And she was no longer *within* the world, watching the path and all the lovely countryside unroll itself beneath her bicycle tires; she was Beryl-the-Author, and everything about that glorious day no longer shone in its simplicity. It would be noted and catalogued and used, somehow, somewhere, in this book or the next. And there were words to be written and a deadline— How could she have forgotten the deadline? Her editor was eager for the book; indeed, there had been a letter from him only the day before, civil, even friendly, but also quite interested in *how soon we might expect &c.*—and still she had that intractable problem with Chapter Six that made everything afterward feel broken and contrived, and why her heroine did not yet suspect the villain, and all those weary words yet to find—

Almost, she might have wept.

But she was a sensible creature. She broke the pottery crock against the oak tree's trunk so that it would return to mud with the rain, and shook out and repacked everything else, and returned to her bicycle. And as she rolled south again, she grew calmer, and grateful for even a half-holiday. The Novel was not often so generous. And after a bit it began to absorb her, and she stopped seeing the world around her pass. Perhaps there was a way to make the attack by smugglers feel a little less coincidental? Perhaps the wicked Marquis might be seen doing something ambiguously sinister earlier? The day was not entirely gone; she might still get some good words written this evening, after tea, when the parlor had cooled down a little.

But some small part of her fought still. Just past the canal, she thought suddenly of the willow-bramble. *I will see it*, she thought rebelliously and then said aloud, "I *will*," as though to the world and her desk in the parlor. There was a turnoff overhung to the very ground with the willow's heavy branches. She pushed her bicycle through the osiers and down to the water's edge, and stood there for a few moments, looking across the River towards the eastern bank, the shining green of reeds and the gleaming brown of drying mud: and a hint, behind a tangle of sedges, of a little lagoon filled with water lilies.

The River chuckled still, generous, undemanding, as though to say, *Never mind, dear heart. I am here. Novels come and go, but until the world itself ends, I remain.*

Chapter Four
A Regrettable Consequence

After the tea party, the Rabbit was much at Toad Hall. Before she and Beryl had gone home, the Toad had invited them both to "drop in whenever you like for potluck. We Toads keep open house! Either of you, or both, whichever you like—for I view you as quite one of the chaps"—a sentiment that caused the Badger to shake his head in disapproval, the Mole to groan softly, and the Water Rat audibly to grind his teeth. And it was as bad as they might have imagined, for the very next day, while Beryl was busy (as she always was in the morning), the Rabbit slipped out of Sunflower Cottage and called upon the Toad, to thank him in person for his lovely party. The Toad, not an early riser, welcomed her with coffee, bacon, devilled kidneys, eggs, toast, muffins, and grapefruits in the breakfast parlor; and liberated from the regulating influence of his friends, his tales, never very close to the truth, grew so outrageous that only the most credulous of listeners could possibly believe them.

But such was the Rabbit. She was delighted, aghast, agog; and they spent nearly the entire day together. He showed her the Library's many *objéts* of interest, following up with a visit to the ruined caravan and motor-car gathering dust in Toad Hall's stables, and to the crumpled wager-boat in the boathouse. The tales he told her strained the laws of probability and even, sometimes, of physics. The Toad (according to himself) was a Hero, plain and simple: clever, cunning, and courageous; dashing, daring, and dangerous to his foes; bold, brave, and beneficent. He faced every challenge fearlessly and with panache. He was a great traveller, an adventurer, the very devil at sport (this said without irony), and a wizard with machines. Taking his words at their face value, the Rabbit could not be faulted for seeing him as a sort of mix of Childe Harold, T. E. Lawrence, and George Stephenson; and if she did not end that first conversation thinking he had himself invented the motor-car, it is not because the Toad did not strongly imply it.

From here things went from bad to worse. While the Toad loved the River Bank and valued his friends greatly, he had often felt the lack of a truly sympathetic companion— by which he meant someone who would listen willingly to his worst exaggerations and affect to believe his boasting. The Rabbit was a sort of dream come true, and he made the most of her company, day after day, until it became an understood thing that she would wander over immediately after breakfast (if Beryl did not want her) and spend the long daylight hours with the Toad.

And added to all the rest was a soupçon of something new to him: envy. The Rabbit was impressed by everything he told her and becomingly reticent about her own life, but when he did pause at last and, remembering his manners, asked her to tell him a bit about herself, her disclosures caused in him little spurts of jealousy. Hot-air balloons? How had *he* not messed about with hot-air balloons before this? *Bank robberies,* forsooth? How was it that *he* had never chanced to be walking along in front of a bank at the very moment of a robbery and then found himself (as had happened with the Rabbit, according to her tale) swept along with the criminals into their getaway car and from thence to their hideout, all quite by accident? It was not that he *wanted* to be arrested and incarcerated again, not precisely—though he had gotten out of that magnificently, had he not? Why, no prison in England could hold the notorious Toad!—but it seemed a bit thick that a mere female (and a Rabbit at that) should have experienced things that had never come his way.

This growing acquaintance blossomed in something like solitude. It was the middle of summer, the sort of glowing, beautiful July when every day is filled with activities, and even the short nights are as apt to be spent fishing or boating or walking about as in checking up on one's neighbors. Immediately after the Toad's tea party, the Badger had returned to the Wild Wood. When he had come to the River Bank to remind the Toad of his social responsibilities, he had left important work undone at home—a Marten had come from the north for an extended visit to some distant relatives, which had riled the Stoats, who were growing restless again and needed settling down; otherwise, who knew what might come of it?—and in any case, he became impatient when separated too long from his beloved Wood.

The Water Rat and the Mole were deep in preparations for a boating expedition upriver, something they expected to take a week or even more, and which therefore required all sorts of unexpected supplies such as rubber rafts (in case of shipwreck) and a small cannon (in case of pirates). The Otter had made his summer's goal to teach his son Portly to swim as well as he did himself, and they were in and out of the River a dozen times a day. The Otter had promised to take Portly to the seashore in

August if he became proficient, and Portly was taking this very seriously.

As for Beryl, she was occupied during that glorious July with work that kept her inside Sunflower Cottage. If she thought of the Rabbit's frequent absences at all, it was with relief, assuming she was entertaining herself with new friends in the neighborhood—which was quite true, though not quite in the way that Beryl meant.

And so it was some weeks before anyone noticed how much time the Rabbit and the Toad were spending together, and by that time, the damage had been done. All the hard work that had gone into rehabilitating the Toad was undone, and he was, once again, an unmanageable ass.

"Toad is turning into an unmanageable ass again," the Water Rat said. "Something must be done."

It was a conclave. Late the night before, he and the Mole had returned at last from their river cruise, a bit sunburnt but otherwise undamaged. The Water Rat had exchanged a word with the Otter, himself just off for his visit to the seaside with Portly, and from him he had learned of this regrettable backsliding. The Toad and the Rabbit had been overheard as they walked along the river-path, discussing motor-boats: their attractiveness—speed—charm—not for beginners, O no indeed, but for the experienced water-animal, nothing could be simpler—and not so very expensive, when one considered their utility: the Toad doing most of the speaking, of course, and the Rabbit only nodding and twittering agreement whenever he was obliged to pause for breath.

Only two days later, the Toad and the Rabbit had spent several hours in the stables looking over the ruined motor-car, the Rabbit making long lists in her beautiful copperplate of the parts that would need repair or replacement, and the Toad repeating, whenever she asked a question, "No, the motor-car must be replaced entirely; that is the only *real* economy."

And a day after that, it had been motor-cycles, after a telegram-messenger had roared up to Toad Hall with a sound that had silenced all the birds and set every dog barking for miles round. The Toad had not even read the telegram, only let it drop to the graveled drive, his eyes round as saucers and very nearly as big. The Rabbit, with her paw over her mouth, exclaimed again and again, "How loud, how . . . splendid! O—my!"

And hearing of this, the Rat had sent off on the double to the Badger to request his *immediate* aid. The Badger had arrived that morning. They were all three extremely tired—the night had been short and too hot for comfortable sleep, and Badger had had rather a walk on top of it—and the day's heat was climbing towards its fiery height. The sun blazed pitilessly down, and the reflections on the River were shatteringly bright where they struck the eye. The air smelt like petrol and plum-pudding just out of the boiler. It was, in fact, the perfect day for sitting with friends upon the Bank, drinking the Rat's ginger beer from mugs as one trailed one's toes in the River, and chatting about nothing in particular—not at all the sort of day for deciding anything important, and *especially* not the kind of day one wanted to waste determining what was to be done (again) about the Toad.

"It's all Beryl's doing," the Mole said, a little grumpily. "We had settled him down nicely, and then she brings this Rabbit among us and sets everything to sixes and sevens again. The Toad was quite a reformed character until *she* came."

"Now, Moley," said the Rat reproachfully. "She is not at all responsible for her friend's doings, any more than *I* have stolen a motor-car, or *you* have been to prison, or Badger here has dressed as an old washerwoman." (The Badger looked startled and a bit indignant.) "Moley, you rag on Miss Mole all the time and I have never understood why. Perhaps it is the heat. It is making everyone short-tempered."

"She brought the Rabbit," the Mole reminded him.

"She did bring the Rabbit," said the Water Rat fair-mindedly, "but how could she know how susceptible Toad is?"

The Badger shook his head. "No, Mole. We cannot blame this young Rabbit. The Water Rat and I have known Toad much longer than you, and I am sorry to say he *doesn't* reform—not for long, anyway. If it were not the Rabbit, it would be something else, and if it were not today, it would be tomorrow or next year."

The Mole might have been overheard to mutter, "Sufficient unto the day is the evil thereof," but the Badger, busy with his thoughts, only continued.

"I have an idea," said he. "Miss Mole is a sensible Mole— quite like yourself, my dear chap—and she may have some influence on her friend. Let us see whether by putting our heads together we may come up with some way to moderate this friendship, so ruinous to the good sense of both."

The Water Rat nodded. "An excellent idea! I suppose it might seem a bit rude, but as the Badger here says, Miss Mole seems a sensible creature. She'll know it's because we're worried about our friend, and not mere impertinence. She's one of us now, so I am sure she doesn't want the sort of trouble Toad gets into any more than we do. If she can encourage the Rabbit to refrain from egging him on (but we won't use that language, 'cos it's low), then we chaps may talk Toad back into a proper frame of mind, and all will be well again."

"For a while," the Badger interjected.

"For a while," the Water Rat agreed. "And we will be sure to be very tactful and proper and polite when we speak to her, so as not to offend her—why, you're the man for that, Moley! You're the very soul of diplomacy."

"A sound plan," the Badger said, and stood. "Shall we go?"

"What, *now?*" said the Rat. It was, as has been mentioned, a hot day, and he rather felt that all this brainwork had earned everyone the rest of the day off.

"Yes, *now,*" said the Badger sternly. "I see your thoughts, Rat, but it cannot be. You and I and the Mole might choose to spend our day quietly, but how can we be sure that the Toad is similarly inclined? Even now, he may be telephoning into Town to purchase some costly machine that he shall inevitably crash in some spectacular fashion."

The Water Rat leapt to his feet, whiskers trembling. "Badger, you are quite right! It doesn't bear thinking of. Come on, Mole." He reached a paw down.

"No," said the Mole.

"No?" said the Rat. "Are you thinking later in the day would be better?"

I mean, no. I will not talk to her!" said the Mole peevishly. "I will *not* be tactful and polite and call on Beryl, and I am sorry, Ratty, to disappoint you, and you, too, Badger, but even if it makes me not such a *parfit gentil* Mole, I will not do it."

"Three is probably too many, anyway," said the Water Rat, only half attending. "Moley, if you're busy, Badger and I will do it ourselves."

Leaving the mystery of the Mole's stubborn refusal (and the Mole) behind them, the Water Rat and the Badger walked down to the river-path. It was not far to Sunflower Cottage, scarcely five minutes along the narrow little walkway beside the purple loosestrife, but quite long enough for the Rat to look upon his

River and gauge its mood. Today it was serene, magisterial; only the passage of a bottle from upstream showed that it ran on strong as ever beneath its smooth, calm face. They walked up the lawn to the cottage's front door, nearly concealed by the heart-shaped leaves of the lilac trees planted to either side.

The Rabbit was not at home ("Egging Toad on, I'm perfectly certain," said the Water Rat) but Beryl was, and after a very few minutes she met them on the lawn that led down to the River, where she kept some really excellent little wrought-iron chairs for sitting and contemplating, and a table.

"What a pleasure!" she said when she came to them. She was dressed simply and with great neatness, except for a smudge of blue-black ink on her glossy cheek, as though she had absently touched a fountain pen to her face while thinking—which is precisely what it was, for she had been busy writing. "Let us have lemonade—unless you would prefer beer? I know fellows often do on a day like this."

The Badger's already high opinion of her good sense soared, but he said only, "I am afraid we must decline, for this is not a social call."

"O dear," said Beryl. "What has happened?"

The Water Rat said, "It is not *what* has happened so much as what *may* happen, if you follow me," and seeing that she didn't, he elaborated, explaining about Toad and his fads; Toad and his inevitable execution of some dangerous and idiotic action relating to those fads; and Toad and all the distress he caused to his neighbors whenever he did so; ending, "So you see, it is up to us to make him as sensible a Toad as can be. Which is not very," he added despondently.

Beryl nodded and poured out lemonade for herself—and beer for them, for she had been too wise to take the Badger's refusal at its face value. "I do appreciate your candor with regard to your friend's, ah, eccentricities, but I don't see what

I can do about it. My acquaintance with him is only of these short months' duration. Might *you* bring your friend round to a more sensible way of thinking?"

The Badger said, "Toad has never been, shall we say, a stable animal. I will be plain, Miss Mole. He was born a flighty Toad and he remains a flighty Toad. He has often before this proven intractable to the promptings of his friends and of his own higher self—"

The Water Rat inserted, "If he has one, as I sometimes doubt."

"But lately he is grown worse: and it is in *this* that we hope for your assistance. It is your friend, Miss Rabbit. Her admiration has inflamed his already weak intellect. It is inciting every sort of bad behavior."

Beryl smoothed her skirt. "I might say the same, alas. Before we came here, Lottie was—I cannot say a sensible Rabbit, for there are hardly any such—but more sensible than she is now, in any case. But ever since she has met your Mr Toad, she has gone quite adventure-mad. We came to the River Bank for a quiet life, a pleasant life where I might work and she might keep me company, with none of this *wilding* about. Yet here is the Toad, encouraging my friend in every sort of excess. Yesterday"—she lowered her voice—"I heard from Lottie that they have been discussing *motor-cycles*, in a very concrete and specific way."

The Badger burst out, "Motor-cycles! Faugh."

The Water Rat said, "You know your friend, Miss Mole. Toad is irredeemable—we know that—but surely *she* can be reasoned with. Can you ask her not to encourage him?"

"I will speak with her," Beryl said, "but I do not think I can offer advice in any way that would not be both discourteous—though I shall not mind *that*, when so much is at stake—and ineffective. She does not stay with me as a companion, that I may tell her how to behave just as though she were a schoolgirl and I her governess. But . . . " She hesitated a moment. "Gentlemen, I must *also* be frank. She is, as you have perhaps observed, a Rabbit. And Rabbits are invariably frivolous. I do not know whether I shall do any good."

There was a silence. They could all hear a breeze hushing through the chestnut's leaves, so lightly that they could not feel it, and far away the clip!-clip!-clip! of some industrious soul trimming a hedge despite the heat.

The Badger said finally, "Well. I had hoped a Mole of your obvious good sense might exert a calming influence over your friend, but perhaps it is not to be hoped for."

Beryl said with a twinkle of a smile, "And your friend, Mr Mole— Does he exert such an influence over the Toad?"

The Badger eyed her sharply. It was not clear from her tone whether it was demure or dry. "The Mole—" he began a little sternly; but the Water Rat, less sensitive, interrupted him, laughing.

"Moley? O dear me, no. He's brave as a tiger, is Mole— Stoats take to their heels when he approaches—but Toad listens to no one! Except, evidently, Miss Rabbit," he added with a fading chuckle.

The Badger said gravely, "This is no laughing matter, Rat. If motor-cycles are being discussed, there is not a moment to be lost. We must separate the Toad and Miss Rabbit as soon as it can be arranged."

Beryl said, "How may it be done? I cannot return Lottie to her family until Christmas-time at the earliest, and even then. . . ." She paused for a moment, then added diffidently, "To send her back early might cause a breach between her family and my own, and all for nothing more than my dear Rabbit being rather silly. Nor can I leave, alas."

The Badger bowed again. "No one would expect it! But it is just like a Mole to consider so noble a sacrifice, even for a moment." (Beryl blushed.) "No, we have another plan, a final solution, one might say: one we hoped never to put into action."

The Water Rat sighed. "It has come to Sophronia, has it?"

"Do you see another possibility?" the Badger asked him.

Slowly, the Water Rat shook his head. Beryl looked from one animal to the other, a question clear in her bright face. The Rat said slowly, "Toad has an aunt, a formidable old—well, battle-axe, to leave the bark on the word. Sophronia is quite aged but tough as oak and hard as granite, and (what is most germane to our purpose) she lives entirely removed from the world, in a castle somewhere in Scotland, or perhaps it is Northumberland. Somewhere uncivilized like that, in any case."

"How horrible!" exclaimed Beryl, with a shudder. "Northumberland! I would not wish that upon my worst enemy!"

"I wouldn't wish it on a dog," agreed the Water Rat.

"And you have not even met the aunt," said the Badger. "But—motor-cycles, you know. It is inevitable: Toad will purchase one, and he will smash it up, and either he will die (which would be bad), or the fines and lawsuits and court costs will bankrupt his estate and cast the once-proud name of Toad forever into the dirt. You have no idea what trouble it was to clear his name and reputation after the last fiasco."

"We had to pay off *reporters*!" confided the Rat.

The Badger continued, "A second such scandal would sink him utterly. But if the Toad is sent to stay with his aunt for twenty or thirty years (or even longer), he may return older, calmer, chastened—and alive, his character unstained. It is not what we would wish for our friend, but if motor-cycles are being discussed, it is out of our hands. We have no choice. I shall send a wire to her immediately, and we shall speak to Toad as soon as he returns from Town, where he went in to get a tooth drawn—and very sensible, for once, not to whine and carry on and delay it as long as he ever could, the way he usually would."

"Really?" said Beryl. "So is Rabbit also in Town—getting a tooth drawn!"

"O dear," said all three simultaneously.

Chapter Five
The Dustley Turismo X

While none of their friends would have believed it, it truly was a coincidence that the Toad and the Rabbit were gone to Town on the same day.

The Rabbit was, at least initially, blameless. She really was going to get a tooth looked at, for it had been paining her for several days. Oil of Cloves had helped, but her mother had always taught her that teeth were not be trifled with, and so she had dutifully written to Town to make an appointment for that morning, and gone off on an early train with a packet of sandwiches (for after the appointment) and ginger beer in a little basket. After the dentist, she intended to go to the Zoo to see the lions and tigers, before taking the 2:14 from Victoria, returning home in time for a late supper with Beryl. It was a blameless way to spend the day, one no one, not even the harshest critic, could find fault with.

But—the—Toad! From beginning to end of that eventful day, his intentions, behavior, and demeanor were reprehensible, though perhaps entirely predictable to anyone who knew him well.

It all came down to motor-cycles, of course. Toad could not stop thinking of his first sight of the telegram-messenger and his magnificent steed. That glorious object of glittering chrome and shining black paint and glossy leather! The dust, the noise, the smell of oil and petrol! The bystanders scrambling to the side, the dogs racing for the hedges, the motor-car drivers shaking their fists in futile envy, the village constables blowing their whistles to no avail! And the rider himself, a slender deity in dusty goggles and helmet, his road-stained black leather coat and gauntlets powdered with dirt; on his face the disdainful expression of Hermes sent to earth by Zeus to give to some great king a telegram. He sat so casually astride his glorious machine, like the conqueror Alexander upon his noble mount Bucephalus, or Perseus astride the divine Pegasus, or—well, there were all sorts of comparisons possible.

Within a minute of seeing the messenger approach along the drive to deliver the telegram, Toad had envisioned himself in identical garb, identically dusty and identically disdainful, sneering as he threw a leg over an identical motor-cycle (but in red) and drove off in a cloud of smoke. It was a lovely vision, an entrancing vision; and the fact that no amount of dusty leather or shining machinery could make him look like anything but what he was, a corpulent and very silly Toad beyond the first flush of youth, affected him to no degree.

The temptation was too much. That glorious machine! The noise, the smell, the smoke, the bystanders' terror! The clashing poetry of its cylinders, the shrilling song of its wheels as they locked! So much better than a motor-car: no broad windscreen to keep the air from his face; no leather seat, sedate as a settee in a parlor; no low, huddling roof to keep off the rain and the wind. *This* was living! Or would be, anyway. He must have a motor-cycle—he must—he MUST!

But how? He knew his friends of old: dear chaps and touchingly devoted; but unnecessarily restrictive, and often so very wrongheaded in the matter of machines. They would try to stop him, if they had any indication of his intention.

His first thought was to make a telephone call to some vendor of motor-cycles in Town and simply order one delivered, along with such replacement tires, motor-oils, special greases, spoke-tighteners, spark plugs, gauntlets, rain-gear, chauffeurs, and trainers as they might advise. Thus, the motorcycle (and its appurtenances) would arrive suddenly and without warning, like a clap of thunder from a clear summer sky. There might be some tut-tutting and my-dear-chapping, but it would be too late for his well-meaning (but misguided) friends to interfere.

This plan was put into immediate effect. The Toad placed the telephone call, and at first it was practically a love feast. The Toad and the genteel motor-cycle salesman immediately discovered in one another a similarity of temperament and taste that would have made them great friends if it were not for the difference in their status. The purchase was quickly determined upon: the motor-cycle would be the largest, most powerful, and most dangerous possible; the gear would be the most expensive; the chauffeur and trainer, the most arrogant.

It was not until the Toad gave his name and direction that things ran into a block. "Mr Toad!" exclaimed the genteel salesman. "Ah. Mr ... Toad, is it? Of Toad Hall, you say? I am ... sorry to say ... Er, I do regret this, but—"

He went on for quite a while, but in the end, the gist of his words became clear even to Toad. He would not—indeed, *could* not—sell and deliver a motor-cycle and accessories to Mr Toad of Toad Hall. The Toad doubled his offer and then tripled it, but to no avail. After this, he blustered at the genteel salesman's oleaginous manager, and then at the manager's apologetic senior manager, and at last at the owner of the motor-cycle garage himself. But the answer was always the same: no motor-cycle for the Toad. He threatened to find another garage in Town, and purchase there an even larger, even more expensive motor-cycle; and at last the shop's owner (who went by the name of Hiccough-Pemberleigh and who sounded on the telephone as though he were sobbing—as indeed he was, at the thought of all that money lost to him) finally told him the full truth. No one *anywhere* would sell him a motor-cycle. In fact, Mr Toad of Toad Hall was banned by an order of Parliament from buying motor-vehicles ever again.

Toad's crimes and prison-break a year past had marked him in the public eye as a desperate criminal, a villain stained to the very bone and a conscienceless recidivist, and so (under considerable pressure from the Opposition newspapers) a special session of Parliament had been called to address The Toad Matter. After days of listening to weeping witnesses tell tales of his perfidy, the House of Commons rose as one and demanded that The Toad Must Be Stopped. But what to do? It had been proven that gaols could not keep him and fines could not chasten him. At last a proposal was bruited: banning his use of motor-vehicles would at least keep him from endangering the public until such time as he committed another crime—of *course* there would be another crime—of such severity that transportation to Australia (in chains) could at last be ordered. At least, the Parliament's members hoped that transportation was still a thing, though they were the first to admit that they not always *au courant* in contemporary affairs.

The Toad (who never read the newspapers and had missed all of this) heard Mr Hiccough-Pemberleigh's explanation, and wept and wept. So weak, so headstrong and foolish! He had allowed mere motor-cars and petty theft to wreck his chance at the one thing, the *only* thing that might make him happy! He had ended the phone call a ruined Toad. He took to his bed immediately, and called for his attorney to make sure his Will was in order.

Yet, perhaps one might blame the Rabbit for the Toad's visit to Town, after all. She called at Toad Hall the very next morning and was surprised when, instead of being ushered into the sunny breakfast-room to hear of his day's plans from an ebullient Toad, she was led instead along an upstairs corridor and into his glorious bedchamber, where she found him a weakened shadow of his former self, with flannel around his throat (though it was July), and a glass of hartshorn and water clasped in one trembling paw.

"Dear Rabbit," he said in a voice scarcely louder than a whisper. "I am so glad to see you . . . one last time."

"O, are you going to Town, as well?" she said brightly. "Why, I—"

"No," he faltered. His face was pale and stained with tears. "I think . . . my traveling days are behind me now." He coughed, and there was a rattle in it.

Finally recognizing the signs, she exclaimed loudly, "Dear Toad, you are not well!"

The Toad winced. "Please . . . My ears are not what they were. Nor my eyes. . . . Could you pull the curtain a little farther across the window? Though I hardly like to. Perhaps . . . perhaps this will be my last sight of the blue sky," and he heaved so painful a sigh that the Rabbit dropped to her knees beside the bed and took one paw in her own, chafing it gently.

"Toad, you really are ill! Has a doctor been summoned?" she asked. "Is it your teeth? Mine are such a trial! I am going into Town tomorrow to have mine looked at, so—"

"It is not my teeth," he said, a little sharply. He struggled against his weariness for a moment, and then continued. "No. There is no point. It is over, quite . . . over."

"But if it is not your teeth, what has happened?" said the Rabbit. "You were so hale yesterday! Why, you were about to purchase a motor-cycle—"

A great wail interrupted her words; and at last the story all came out, made nearly incoherent by the sobs and the fluttering of lawn handkerchiefs. Certain critical details were omitted—such as the fact that selling him a motor-cycle was now actually illegal, instead of just ill-advised—so it is not surprising that the Rabbit was left thinking that the problem was one of delivery. "There, there," she said, and patted the Toad's paw. "I am sure it is just a misunderstanding. Perhaps, if you could just speak with Mr Hiccough-Pemberleigh face-to-face—"

The Toad sobbed, "Impossible, alas . . . My days of jaunting into Town—gone now; all gone. Never again—"

But suddenly the Toad fell silent, his mouth wide agape and his dull eyes afire with a new idea. He dropped his handkerchief onto the coverlet. "O!" he said after a time, and then, "O, my!" and finally, "Why, yes, perhaps, it might work;" but he explained none of this to the Rabbit. Still, when she left him a few minutes later, she was pleased that he was looking so much better than he had, and was even sitting up in bed, eating toast dipped in weak tea with a thoughtful expression upon his round face.

In any case, the Rabbit was surprised the next morning to find the Toad on the same train into Town.

She was walking along the corridor through the first-class car, peering in a worried fashion into her little reticule, for she had put her second-class ticket somewhere safe (so as not to lose it), and now could not find it—really, she had it a minute ago! How could she have lost it already? Had she put it in her basket? No, not there, and it had not slipped under the sandwiches. . . . O, *there* it was! She had tucked it into the wrist of her glove—and there *he* was suddenly: Toad, one watery eye visible through a crack in the door of a private compartment with its blinds pulled down tightly.

"Why—Toad!" exclaimed the Rabbit with delight. "You look *ever* so much better than yesterday! I did not know you were going into the—"

But the Toad only hissed, "Don't say my name!" and with one desperate paw, he dragged her into the compartment and snapped the door closed behind them. The blinds on the outside windows were shut, as well, and the compartment felt very close. "Not so loud! They might be pursuing me." His expression was quite frenzied.

The Rabbit said, "Why, who? Toad, did you not pay for your ticket?"

"Of course I did!" whispered the Toad indignantly. It was by no means beyond him to try to get by without paying when he had forgotten to take money; but today he *had* paid, and this aspersion upon his character wounded him more than it might upon another day. He dropped his voice. "I mean the Badger and the Water Rat. They might be slinking about the train station, you know—trying to stop me."

The train gave a gentle jerk as it started to roll forward.

"O, no!" said the Rabbit. "I saw them not a quarter of an hour ago, as I was leaving the cottage. They were come to call upon Beryl, but I just slipped away without saying anything, so as not to miss the train."

The Toad threw himself onto one of the seats and mopped his brow with his handkerchief. "Then I am safe! The Toad slips their leash! I am proven yet again a genius, the very model of cunning!" And with a chortle of satisfaction, he popped the blinds, which spun up to expose the countryside, flying past the window faster and faster, and not a single Water Rat nor Badger in sight anywhere.

"Have a seat, have a seat," said the hospitable Toad grandly.

"Well, if you think I should," said the Rabbit; "I have only a second-class ticket. You *do* look so much better than yesterday! Are you going to see a doctor in Town?"

"A doctor? A DOCTOR?" The Toad began giggling with abandon. "That's what *they* all think! Tricked them all! Otter, Badger—everybody else! I told Otter I was coming to town to see the dentist."

"You *too*? Is *that* what was wrong, yesterday? I know you said something about motor-cycles, but I knew it could not be merely that! I did not know you were a fellow sufferer. Why, I could have suggested my own dentist. He is *very* good, and so gentle and polite!" The Rabbit began hunting for the slip of paper with her dentist's address written upon it: in her reticule, in the pocket of her bright, checkered mantelet, in her glove. O, there it was! She had forgotten: Beryl had pinned it to her lapel, so that it could not be lost.

"No, no, no, my dear girl." The Toad grinned widely at her, displaying his complete and proper absence of teeth, so that the Rabbit blushed. "Tricked them all," he gloated again. "No. I am gone into town to look at motor-cycles."

She gasped. "O, *Toad!* Dare you? But the gentleman at the garage! He said—"

"Never mind what he said. I'll walk in—*quite* casually, as though I were a mere window-shopper—ask to see the largest and most beautiful motor-cycle they have—and I shall pay *cash* for it"—he pulled from his brocaded waistcoat a fat roll of bank notes—"and I shall ride it home!"

"O, *Toad!*" she said again. "What a clever idea! There will be no names given, so they cannot deny you! But—can you *ride* a motor-cycle?"

The Toad shrugged his shoulders. "I shall have them show me, but I should imagine it will be much like driving a motor-car. It certainly will not be beyond *me!*"

"Or like a bicycle, perhaps!" said the Rabbit. "Why, they both have two wheels! I am quite an experienced bicyclist— I have my own Lallement Princesse," she said proudly; "and it is shining red, and has the loveliest little basket—"

"Perhaps a bit like a bicycle," said the Toad with a patronizing air. "Red! Of course it must be a *red* motor-cycle, the reddest motor-cycle that ever was."

The Rabbit said, a little sadly, "And I shall miss it all. I shall be having a tooth looked at, and by the time *that* is over, you'll be gone already, off into the countryside in a great roar! I should love to see that."

"You may watch me ride about when you return to the River Bank," said the Toad kindly.

Upon their arrival in Town, the Toad hailed the first hackney cab he saw and was at Hiccough-Pemberleigh Motors in no time at all. It was indeed everything he had dreamed of—a glorious place, an Aladdin's-cave of marvels. The double-doors, so tall, so invitingly open! To the left, the showroom, its large windows offering peeks at the wonders within: here, a reflection of blue sky along a chromium handlebar; there, the twinkle of sunlight sparkling upon a faceted headlamp. To the right side was a garage, its four green doors folded back to offer intriguing glimpses into a gloomy cavern filled with mysterious equipment, all a-bustle with slightly grubby men in mechanics' coveralls. Above it all was a shining dark blue sign that read (in white): HICCOUGH-PEMBERLEIGH MOTORS: MOTOR-CYCLES FOR THE GENTRY.

The Toad strutted into the cool, dark showroom and gazed and gazed, but his reception was disappointing. *There* were the motorcycles, six or seven of them encircled by red velvet ropes draped from brass stands, shining black or green or midnight-blue (but none red, alas); and *there* were the beautifully suited shop-men, five or six of them standing in ornamental clumps at the back of the room, like pampas grass in pots; and *here* was he, Toad of Toad Hall, the rich daredevil, the Toad-about-town! But his *incognito* had its disadvantages: he saw none of the agreeable rushing about he was used to whenever he entered showrooms in his own name.

After it became clear to the beautifully suited shop-men that this unknown caller was not merely going to wander in and then out, one drifted across the room and said, "How may I help you?" in a supercilious tone, with the emphasis just slightly upon the *you*.

The Toad drew himself up to his full height, such as it was. "No, *you* may not! I shall deal with none but your proprietor, for *I* am—" But here he stopped, for he remembered suddenly that Toad of Toad Hall was an unwelcome customer—indeed, illegal. Now the salesman was looking down on him with— could that be contempt? He finished with great pomp, "*I* am Mr Green, the world-famous motor-cyclist."

"Mr Green . . . ?" mused the shop-man, and gestured. Another shop-man separated himself from his fellows, idled across, and looked inquiringly at them both. Said the first, "Mr Gervase, this is the 'famous' Mr Green. The motor-cyclist. Perhaps *you* have heard of him . . . ?" Toad could hear the quotation marks around "famous."

The second shop-man stared down the length of his long nose, inspecting Toad. "Perhaps Mr, ah, Green has found himself in the wrong place?"

"I shall be paying cash," said Toad with a flourish of bank notes.

"O, Mr *Green!*" instantly said both shop-men. "Of course! The *famous* Mr Green!"

After that, things went much more smoothly. Mr Hiccough-Pemberleigh was summoned from his office and appeared, bowing and scraping in the most gratifying manner. The velvet ropes were removed and each motorcycle was in its turn rolled out onto the pavement before the showroom, to glitter and gleam in the sunlight; extolled in the most glowing of language, with enough references to Specifications thrown in to keep it all from feeling entirely like an appeal to Toad's emotions (as in fact it was); inspected; started and listened to; and declared inadequate by the Toad. He paused and considered for a time when he came to the last: the largest, shiniest, loudest, and fastest motor-cycle, a Dustley Turismo X painted a lush dark green that might have reminded the poetically inclined of pine forests in Norway—*not* red, alas—but in the end, even this was rejected.

Then came the moment feared by every purveyor of durable major consumer goods, when the Toad finally said, "So this is all you have?"

"Well...," said Mr Hiccough-Pemberleigh, thinking quickly. "We can of course order others for you from the manufactory—I have many catalogues, if you should like to see them—"

"Paugh," said the Toad.

"—but we have nothing else here, except the red Nonpareil—"

"The Nonpareil!" echoed the sales-men reverently.

"—but that is a racing motor-cycle, sir, not at all suitable for ordinary riding," finished Mr Hiccough-Pemberleigh.

"A racing motor-cycle! Show me the Nonpareil, my good man," said the Toad imperiously. "It is red, you say?"

"*Very* red," Mr Hiccough-Pemberleigh said. "The precise red one generally sees only on the most irresponsible of motor-cars. But I should not even have mentioned it! The Nonpareil is, unhappily, quite impossible. One of the mechanics has been adjusting the carburetor, so it is in the garage, in pieces. It cannot be shown at this time. Perhaps next week."

But the Toad only shook his head emphatically. "No, indeed! Show it to me at once. Why did you not tell me of this *first*, and save us both all this time? A racing motor-cycle, in red! Did you think any of these lesser machines should do for a world-famous motor-cyclist such as myself?"

"But there are pieces off," said Mr Hiccough-Pemberleigh plaintively.

The Toad said, "Then they may be put back on, my good man. I shall wait until your mechanic has finished his adjustments, and in the meantime, we may discuss such supplemental purchases as a leather riding suit, and a helmet, and bags, and—and such. I shall wear the riding suit and helmet, but you may send everything else to—" he nearly said, "Toad Hall," but managed to stop himself; and as the Mole seemed the chap least likely to refuse delivery, he amended it to, "Mr Green, care of Mr Mole, at Mole End, near the River Bank."

Mr Hiccough-Pemberleigh frowned. "The River Bank? There is a notorious Toad who lives just about there."

The Toad smiled his most innocent, most charming smile. "O, *him*. Toad! He is quite a folk-hero on the River Bank, with his daring and his bold feats! Almost a legend, one might say. Quite the great man of those parts. But we don't speak of him," he revised hastily, seeing Mr Hiccough-Pemberleigh's expression. "He is not received anywhere."

It took rather a while for the mechanic to reassemble the bits he had just disassembled (and not without some grumbling, for he loved the Nonpareil the way some grooms love the horses they tend), but the time was spent to the great mutual satisfaction of the Toad and Mr Hiccough-Pemberleigh in the purchasing of everything to do with motor-cycles that could be purchased. There was a hitch in the proceedings, for the Toad also wished to hire a chauffeur to keep his motor-cycle in order, something Mr Hiccough-Pemberleigh was very willing to do for him. Again, the Mole—or rather, his direction—came to the rescue, though he did not know it: the chauffeur might report to Mole End, and then be directed to Toad Hall, at which point (reasoned the Toad) it would be too late for anyone to do anything about it all.

The mechanic had the carburetor reinstalled in somewhat more than a trice but rather less than an hour. The Toad, trying on a riding suit and helmet before a mirror, and rather liking the effect of such a gleaming effulgence of leather, caught the flash of red and chromium from the corner of his eye as the Nonpareil was rolled onto the pavement. He moaned aloud.

"Sir?" said Mr Hiccough-Pemberleigh. "Are you well?"

"O my! O my! That beauty—that angel!" groaned the Toad, and walked from the showroom as though pulled upon a string. There the Nonpareil was before him: a slender, low, lethal-looking motor-cycle; a vain, useless, frivolous object (very like the Toad himself, in character if not conformation); a machine emphatically red. It managed to convey a sense of imprudent speed even though it was standing quite still.

"How—how does it start?" said the Toad, licking his lips, for they were dry. He felt his heart flutter in his breast: never had anything been as beautiful as the Nonpareil!

The mechanic frowned a little. "I thought you was a great motor-cyclist, sir. The Nonpareil, she's a beauty all right, but she starts same as all the other motorcycles. You climb on and then you tickle the carburetor—like this, sir—and then you—"

But it was too late. At the mechanic's first words, the Toad had heaved himself up onto the leather saddle, his paws just reaching the handlebars and his toes just reaching the foot-pegs. All words of advice and admonishment went unheard as he cried, "Stand aside!", rolled on the accelerator, and released the clutch. The Nonpareil leapt forward into the road, where it immediately hit a cobble and fell. The Toad leapt clear as the Nonpareil skittered along the road upon its side, leaving a trail of foot-pegs, cables, gear-levers, valve-covers, dark fluids, and unidentifiable bits of metal.

A dozen anguished voices went up at once: "The Nonpareil!"

By virtue of his shape, the Toad rolled some little distance before bumping to a stop against the wheels of a perambulator where it stood outside a milliner's shop, which set the infant inside to crying. Mr Hiccough-Pemberleigh and the mechanic rushed across to where the Toad lay winded but quite uninjured, and grabbed him.

Mr Hiccough-Pemberleigh cried, "Mr Green! Are you all right, sir?"

But the mechanic shouted to a bystander, "'Ere, you! Call a constable! 'E oughter be up on charges for ruinin' a valuable motor-cycle!"

The infant in the perambulator was howling, a remarkably full-bodied sound for so small an article.

Mr Hiccough-Pemberleigh exclaimed, "Mike, of course we're not going to summon the police! Mr Green shall pay for the repairs, that's all."

The Toad, who had been thinking quickly, groaned artistically and opened an eye. "Where ... am I?" he managed in a feeble croak.

"Sir, you are alive!" exclaimed Mr Hiccough-Pemberleigh joyfully. "Can you sit up? You—"

"The Nonpareil—something was . . . wrong with it," gasped out the Toad. He looked reproachfully (yet weakly) at the mechanic.

"There was not!" exclaimed the mechanic, recoiling. "H'it was h'in perfect running order."

"There was," said the Toad, more robustly. Mr Hiccough-Pemberleigh was looking between the two of them doubtfully. To clinch the deal, the Toad went on, "As a world-famous motor-cyclist, I know these things. The carburetor was assembled improperly."

"H'it was not!"

"Sir—" said Mr Hiccough-Pemberleigh.

At this moment, the squalling infant's nurse ran from the milliner's shop. She had meant to leave her charge for a mere moment, to try on a hat that had caught her eye in the front window, a really very charming bonnet with a plaid ribbon and rosettes, suitable for half-days off. The hat had not suited; but there had been another, nearly as charming, and then a third, rather more so—and she had allowed herself to be drawn into a discussion of the merits of pigeon feathers on close bonnets, or whether they might be a bit quaint. Things had rather developed from there. But she had kept one eye upon the pram just outside, and now she shouldered her way through the tangle of men and motor-cycle parts to snatch up her squalling charge.

She cooed, "Ooh, is Baby afwaid? Has Baby been scared by the nasty mens?" She glared: the very model of a modern nurse, with the obligatory hatchet-jaw and discreet black dress and white apron—though the effect was somewhat countered by the hat on her head, fashioned of improbably yellow straw surmounted by ostrich feathers dyed fern- and olive-green, and a yellow-and-olive gingham ribbon.

"Obviously I shall not take a defective Nonpareil!" said the Toad with great firmness. "*And* I shall not pay for the repairs. Indeed, you are lucky no more serious damage was done, and that I am choosing not to press charges."

Madame Celeste—for that was the milliner's name, to judge by the sign over her shop—emerged, calling in an exaggerated French accent. "My 'at, madame! *Mon bon chapeau!*"

"'Ere, what?" exclaimed the mechanic.

"Ze nasty mens, with their loud voices!" said the nurse reproachfully to the infant. It was still crying.

"My 'at!" again shrieked Madame Celeste. "Remove eet at once, madame, at *once!* Zis is theft!"

"For allowing me to drive off on a defective vehicle," the Toad explained to Mr Hiccough-Pemberleigh. "No one would be surprised if I found it necessary to file a lawsuit for injuries sustained—" He coughed experimentally.

"Ooh, sir . . .," interjected Mr Hiccough-Pemberleigh in agony.

The nurse glared at Madame Celeste, but only cooed to the child, "Ooh, the hat-lady is nasty, is she? Baby is taking up all of Nursey's attention, and the nasty hat-lady will just have to wait until Baby is all quiet, won't she, my precious?"

The Toad continued, "But I am a magnanimous individual. My friends say I am too forgiving, but there it is. I'll take *that* one instead." He gestured at the dark-green Dustley Turismo X.

"The Dustley?" said the mechanic and Mr Hiccough Pemberleigh in unison.

Madame Celeste reached across and tried to tug the hat from the nurse's head, who threw up one hand to protect herself, as there were a number of hatpins holding it in place. There ensued a tussle.

"Yes," said the Toad, "at once! It is not red, and it is not the Nonpareil"—and here a tear welled in one eye—"but"—and here he perked up—"it is nevertheless a glorious machine. Fast, you say?"

"Very," Mr. Hiccough-Pemberleigh assured him with dawning hope, pushing the nurse and milliner out of his way.

"And dangerous, I daresay?" said the Toad casually.

The mechanic said, "H'in your 'ands, *very* 'azardous. But wot about the ruin of this 'ere Nonpareil?"

"And such a lovely green," added Mr Hiccough-Pemberleigh hurriedly, and tittered. "Why, it is quite your namesake!"

The Toad said, "What? O, I see," and began, regtrettably, to giggle. "Yes, I'll take this motor-cycle, the Dustley, but I expect a discount for it."

This is where matters stood—unpromising but not yet ruinous—when the Rabbit appeared upon the scene, and said, "O no! Mr Toad, are you injured?"

The Rabbit's tooth had been looked at but it had not needed to be drawn, after all: a few minutes' filing and some Wintergreen Oil, and it was done. The Rabbit felt immediately better. The sandwiches had been eaten upon a curved-metal and wooden bench at the park, where she watched a man standing upon a box and declaiming loudly. He was either for the Government or against it, she could not tell exactly which; but whichever it was, he was incensed. When she was done, she folded up her napkin neatly and tucked it back into the basket. She looked at her little lapel-watch. The dentist had taken longer than she had expected, but there was still time to see the lions and tigers and penguins at the Zoo. And so off she went.

She had nearly forgotten about the Toad's purchase when she hurried up from the Underground near the Zoo and saw, immediately across the street, a shining dark-blue sign that read (in white): HICCOUGH-PEMBERLEIGH MOTORS: MOTOR-CYCLES FOR THE GENTRY. A row of motorcycles glistened upon the pavement in front of the shop, and a number of ornamental shop-men were clustered gleaming in the shop's doorway; but her attention was drawn immediately to the wreckage of what looked as though it might once have been a red motor-cycle. Two men led a drooping third figure away from it: a small figure, quite a squat figure, dressed in tight leather, with a brown leather helmet jammed down upon his round head: unmistakably the Toad!

The Toad had been in a motor-cycle accident! The Rabbit hurried across the busy street, and as soon as she was close enough, she called out, "O no! Mr Toad, are you injured?"

Fateful words, infelicitous words! Mr Hiccough-Pemberleigh dropped the Toad's arm and staggered back as though he had been stung by a wasp; but the mechanic only tightened his grip. "'Ere, what?" said he again: "Mr *Toad*, h'is h'it? The desprit criminal? A-ruining my beautiful Nonpareil? *An'* tryin' to buy this 'ere Dustley?"

Rabbit recognized her misstep. "O! But you are *not* Mr Toad at all, are you? I am so sorry for mistaking you! You are quite another person, and I only mistook you for him. Indeed—" She turned prettily to Mr Hiccough-Pemberleigh, who had seated himself upon his shop's low windowsill and was turning a gentle shade of green. She laid a paw on his sleeve. "Why, he is not even a little similar. Mr Toad is quite tall, and very distinguished! I don't see how I can have made that mistake, but I am very nearsighted, you know."

"Now, see here, miss," said the mechanic, giving the quivering Toad a shake. "H'it's 'im, right enough! I can tell, now's you says h'it, from the police-circular. Lots of young ladies gives their 'earts to desprit criminals, but 'e's not worth h'it, missy, not by a long chalk. H'it's the gallows for 'im!"

And just at this moment, the Rabbit and the Toad heard the sounds they wanted to hear least in this world: a constable's whistle and the footsteps of a heavyset policeman approaching at a lumbering trot. Everyone looked towards the sound—and in that instant of inattention, the Toad, with rare quickness of thought, acted. He ripped his arm from the mechanic's slackened grasp. "Ha, ha!" he cried, and leapt upon the saddle of the Dustley Turismo X. Quite amazingly, the motor-cycle started at the first try—not for nothing was the Dustley widely praised for its dependability—and he spun the motor-cycle in a circle, its wheels kicking stones at the shop-men and cracking one of the enormous windows. "Ho, ho! I tricked you all! 'Mr Green'—there is no such creature! All a ruse! Yes, I am HE—the clever Toad, the devious Toad! You wouldn't sell ME a motor-cycle, would you? And yet here I am!"

Recovering from his shock, the mechanic lunged at the Dustley, but the Toad with a gay laugh rode straight at him. The man threw himself to the side, colliding with a constable who had just puffed up shouting, "'Ere, 'ere, wot's all—" They went down onto the cobbles in a sort of *mâçedoine* of limbs, bystanders, perambulators, and broken Nonpareil parts.

The Toad veered, recovered, and was past! He paused a moment to throw a final taunt over his shoulder, though the specifics were lost in the roar of the engine. The Rabbit took the opportunity to fling herself onto the saddle behind the Toad. The police constable heaved upright and threw himself toward them, but it was too late. The Dustley, the Toad, and the Rabbit were gone in a flurry of dust, smoke, and bank notes and guineas, as the Toad threw the money for the motor-cycle (and gear) into the air behind him.

The Toad accelerated away from the crime scene. "Ha, ha! I get away with another daring deed!" He turned left-hand into an alley, narrowly avoiding a stray dog. "The Toad, too dangerous to be permitted near motor-cycles?" He bumped out of the alley onto a major street. "Dangerous, yes! But I find a way!"

He turned right-handed, and veered to avoid a hansom cab. The horse rose in its traces: it was all too used to the indignities of London life, but this—a Toad and a Rabbit, *clearly* from the country, riding a large motor-cycle at unsafe speeds—was Just Too Much. If Town was going to be overrun by joy-riding rural hooligans, then perhaps it was time for a decent, hard-working cab horse to retire.

The Rabbit had rearranged herself as well as she could whilst thundering over cobblestones and swerving around sharp corners. She was now straightened out behind him, her skirts pulled neatly close and her arms as far around his girth as they could reach. She had lost her basket, alas, but was relieved to note that her reticule still hung from her wrist, though it was flying about on the end of its cords in a way that did not bode well for its long-term security. Still, there was nothing she could do about it just now, and her mother had always said that there was no reason to borrow trouble from tomorrow; and so she peeped over his shoulder instead.

Certainly there was more than enough *immediate* trouble to fill a Rabbit's dance card! The Toad was jolting along a busy street, inserting the motor-cycle between two lanes of traffic that seemed composed entirely of large omnibuses that loomed over them, lined with startled faces staring down as they careened past. But it was all so thrilling, everything whirring by at a great pace. *There*, a churchyard narrowly avoided! *There*, a fruit-stand evaded by inches! *There*, a Jubilee fountain circumvented, so close that the spray got into her fur! The blast of air in her face quite took her breath away, and she found she had to fold back her ears to keep it from rushing into them and deafening her.

"Ho, ho," chortled the Toad, never able to keep his mouth closed for long. "What a clever Toad I am—too clever for shop-men, too clever for shop-owners! Too clever for mechanics and constables! The cleverest Toad that ever was— Brains will tell! Banned from exercising my right to purchase dangerous machinery—I find a way! Barred from operating it at high speeds on public thoroughfares—yet here I am!"

Just ahead, there was an opening in the buildings clustering close around them: a public square, with a little low stone wall surrounding it and memorial archways for entrances: inside, a plethora of statues and a fountain with bronze dolphins, and a great many people walking about. With a wicked laugh, the Toad zipped through a gap between omnibuses and up a shallow flight of stairs ("O, o, o, o, o!" exclaimed the Rabbit) and beneath an archway, onto the square itself, among the pedestrians.

But the Toad had the bit truly in his teeth by now. He shouted, "I am Toad, THE Toad, the desperate and dangerous Toad!" He turned neither to the left nor the right, but roared straight across the square—though it should also be acknowledged that he was still quite inexperienced with motor-cycles, and would in any case have been unable to turn abruptly without a tumble. Pigeons, nannies, dogs, chestnut vendors, and perambulators flew in every direction. "Ha, ha!" laughed the Toad. "Like ninepins!"

But there again came a sound horrid to the ear, rising above the shrieks and screams: O dread! It was *another* constable's whistle, ominous and shrill, and with it came the feared cry, "'Alt! 'Alt in the name of the Law!" And then a second whistle joined the first—and a third! The Rabbit glancing behind them saw any number of constables rushing along in their wake, constables of every size and fitness-level. "They're after us!" she exclaimed.

The Toad glanced back and laughed. "Let them shout! Let them bellow! Let them whistle 'til they're blue! They cannot catch me! I—I am the unstoppable Toad, the master of the roads, the very devil of machines! Let them curse their curses, and set their traps— I shall escape them all!"

But then came the worst sound of all, the siren of a police motor-car as it screeched to a halt—*and it was in front of them!*—in fact, in the archway just ahead, precisely where they needed to be leaving the square.

"Ha, ha!" said the Toad, but a little less certainly.

"O, be careful!" cried the Rabbit. The Toad's attention was all for the constables behind and ahead, but *she* saw that a cluster of young ladies had walked directly into his path, laden with the fruits of their morning's shopping. The Toad veered, and young ladies, bandboxes, and parcels tumbled out of his way. Things got worse! A *second* police motor-car joined the first in the archway, leaving only a foot or two between their headlamps. Constables began to pour from every door.

"Ho, ho," said the Toad, but it was clear his heart was no longer in it.

"No, do not slow down!" said the Rabbit, for the Toad was suddenly drooping in his seat, and the first fat tears were rolling down his face and flying back to splash her fur.

"No, I see it now!" sobbed the Toad and slowed a little more. "We are trapped, we are doomed! Every gate secured—

We shall never escape! We shall be hauled to prison and kept there for a hundred years, or even two. Chains, bread and water, the noose, then drawn and quartered! How has my life come to this? If only I were not such an unfortunate Toad, such a luckless Toad!"

The Toad gave a great sob and slowed still further. The pursuing constables gave a breathless cheer (it is no easy matter to pursue a motor-cycle on foot through a crowd, even if one is not corpulent, as many of the constables were) and catching their second (or, in some cases, third) wind, spurred forward after him. The constables from the motor-cars in the archway smiled with fell intent: it was universally known that to capture the notorious Toad would mean a promotion and a raise, and two week's holiday at the seaside at the taxpayers' expense.

"Alas!" wept the Toad.

But the Rabbit pinched him sharply about his middle, causing him to straighten suddenly and the motor-cycle to swerve, conveniently avoiding a nun incautiously leading a double file of small girls in yellow hats across their path. "You are *not* an unlucky Toad! You make your own luck!"

The Toad perked up slightly.

"It is simple," said the Rabbit into his ear—and quite sensibly, if one thinks about it; "If you do not wish to go to gaol, then do not get caught!"

"Of course!" cried the mercurial Toad. "Such a simple yet ingenious solution! Don't—get—CAUGHT! Genius! I should have thought of it in another moment, but you did very well, Rabbit!"

"If you think so," said the Rabbit modestly; but the Toad did not reply, for he was once again a Toad of action and decision. He sped up, and aimed the Dustley for the gap between the two police motor-cars. Surely it was too narrow! Surely they would be stopped! But the Toad was not deterred—there was room enough—and as he swept through the space between the machines, he sketched a mock bow from the saddle of the Dustley. This most unfortunately meant he removed one paw from the handlebar and the motor-cycle swerved in response. Seeing his opportunity, a constable made a quick grab—but to no avail, for the Rabbit only clung tighter to the Toad and pushed the man away with one of her little boots. It was nothing so unladylike as a kick; still, the constable fell to the ground with a howl, clutching his central region and gnashing his teeth.

And they were past! The Toad raced along a thoroughfare, trailing police motor-cars and pedestrian constables. A right, a left, another right; a narrow alley; another park; through the archway of an inn and out into the mews. The Toad (with Rabbit) surged through the crowded streets, and the crowds fled from his thundering approach—sometimes with intemperate haste that led them headfirst into rubbish bins or sprawling through the open doors of startled but not unwilling shops, at which the Toad rather inconsiderately laughed. The weight of the Rabbit behind him was an inconvenience, as he suspected she slowed down the motor-cycle somewhat, but at least she did not squeal and scream as many females might have, and more than once she did good yeoman work, deflecting enterprising pedestrians with her foot. The sirens and whistles behind them faded until they were gone, the last of the police motor-cars fallen far behind.

But the Toad did not slow down, not for anything. The found themselves in a section of the Town devoted to industry, where factories coughed black smoke into the sky, and the Rabbit had to squeeze her eyes shut against the cinders in the air. The Toad, who was wearing the helmet and goggles from Hiccough-Pemberleigh, was not deterred but tore along roads cluttered with heavy horse-drays and motor-trucks that spewed thick gray fumes. Under the Dustley's wheels, Town turned into suburbs, mile after mile of semi-detached villas and poorly maintained parks, and cricket-greens turned brown with neglect.

"How do they live like this?" the Rabbit exclaimed aloud suddenly.

The Toad had been maintaining a steady monologue of the sort of self-praise that rapidly becomes too tedious to record; but he heard this and paused in his peroration. "What's this you say?" he asked, tipping his round head a little to one side.

"Don't stop looking at the street!" cried the Rabbit, for they were entering a little shopping district of tobacconists and chemists and bookshops and ironmongers, all grubby and rundown and rather crowded. "The people, I mean. Everything so—dreary! Even the trees look drab." And she was right, for the elms and poplars and oaks looked dusty and dry.

"They must like it!" said the Toad, sober for once. "Why else would they stay?"

"I don't see how they *can* like it," she said. "They must be *forced* to stay, somehow. Perhaps it is this *work* one is always hearing about. It must be a thing one may only do in the Town."

"Ah, *work*," said the Toad, as though he too had heard of it. "It makes them slow, anyway," and he began chortling again. "Too slow to catch *me*! Too fast for any of them! Lightning, thunder! A hurricane!" And he was off again.

The suburbs gave way to the calm, glowing afternoon countryside. A wide lane opened out in front of him. It was too much to expect restraint after he had been trammeled all that while by narrow streets and cobbles and crowds. He let himself go, and the motorcycle leapt forward in a cloud of dust.

The Rabbit gave an involuntary squeak and tightened her grasp.

"Ow, stop pinching!" cried he over his shoulder. "You saw it all! A witness to my triumph, my glory!"

"Yes, Toad!" she shouted over the wind. "Tell me—"

But the Toad was on a roll. "Ho, ho! Who escapes from every trap? Toad: only Toad! Who slips from their grasp, yet again? Why, they all cry, 't is Toad! They may try to catch me on this glorious motor-cycle, but it can't be done! Again and again, I slip through their fingers! He, he! Sly as a Fox and twice as smart!"

The Rabbit could see over the Toad's shoulder. Set back from the road a bit to their right, was a pub: not a smart carriage-trade inn, but a sensible country pub, with decent beer and the smell of pipe-smoke like a miasma about it. A furlong or two in front of them, the lane branched suddenly to the left and right. "Now what?" she shouted.

"Toad, the terror of the highways! Toad, the— Which way?" he said, in quite a different tone.

The Rabbit said only, "Where to? Do we stop?"

The Toad slowed a little.

In the end, the decision was taken from them. Every respectable country pub has a dog to keep an eye upon things, and this pub was typical in this, and also in the size, speed, and vociferousness of the dog, and in its strongly held opinions about the right of easement to be granted any given passerby. Large motor-cycles controlled imperfectly by Toads in riding kit, with Rabbits in walking-dress seated pillion, were *not* part of the proper order of things, and the fact that the motor-cycle was slowing down *as though it might stop*, pushed the whole thing entirely beyond the pale. Seeing its duty clear, the dog leapt to its feet and came out of the innyard at a dead run, barking and howling. The Toad gave a little scream and accelerated abruptly, twisting his ponderous torso to track the dog's progress. The Rabbit cried, "Watch out!"

It was too late. The Toad hit the signpost head-on. The Dustley crumpled. The Toad and the Rabbit tumbled over its handlebars, head over heels, into a blackberry bramble that had grown up in the ditch just there. The dog raced up and began barking and sniffing. Its goal, to capture and utterly annihilate the motor-cycle, had been rendered moot; but surely some entertainment still might be gleaned from this! If only these cursed brambles were not in the way, there would be a chance of snatching up one of these wretched riders in its jaws and shaking him for a while.

With great presence of mind, the Rabbit dragged the Toad (who was no help at all, entirely caught up in rolling about, clutching his head, and moaning, "O my! O woe!" before he fell into a deep swoon) deeper into the bramble. The dog, a country dog and therefore pragmatic, soon saw that there was no prospect of fulfilling its ambitions and returned to the inn, leaving the hapless motor-cyclists to their fate.

Chapter Six
Water Lilies

At the little writing-desk in the parlor, Beryl laid down her fountain pen with a sigh of satisfaction. She had wrought hard and well all that morning. Her villain's machinations had hitherto been a source of dissatisfaction for her, as though they existed solely to give the heroine something to be confounded by (and what possible motivations could justify acts so irrational, so contrary to the villain's stated objectives?); but a solution had come to her in the night—perhaps the villain was mad! What could be better?—and Beryl had spent several fevered hours writing a scene set in Bedlam to be inserted into an earlier chapter, which would Establish His Character; and now she felt that momentary, delightful, smug mental fatigue which comes when one has worked hard before lunch and the rest of the day may with a clean conscience be given over entirely to lesser, less wearying tasks.

As she neatly squared off the new pages, she looked from the window beside her desk. The day was, again, beautiful—for this was a beautiful summer, a perfect summer, as though the River Bank were bent on showing its best side to its new residents. What might she do? Why, anything—but it did seem as though drinking lemonade and reading adventure novels (as research) in a hammock slung from the chestnut tree would be a productive use of her afternoon. Or that might be too close to the river path; for people were always passing and some of them would want to talk to her.

But what was this? She saw to her astonishment the figures of the Badger and the Water Rat marching up her lawn from the river path, with the Mole trailing a few steps behind, looking unhappy. The Badger held a newspaper in one hand. She went out to them.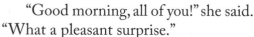

"Good morning, all of you!" she said. "What a pleasant surprise."

"Not for long," said the Water Rat grimly.

"Have you read this morning's newspapers from town?" said the Badger without preamble.

"I have been working," she said with private pride, "but we do not get any newspapers here, in any case. Why, what has happened? Is it the Rabbit?" she added, in sudden alarm. "She did not come home last night. Has something happened to her?"

"She's *not* here, then," said the Badger.

Beryl said, "I thought that her bad tooth perhaps required a second visit, and that she might have stayed at her club in Town and forgotten to send me a telegram. That is exactly the sort of thing she would do."

The Water Rat burst out, "Then it is all true!"

"Rat, we don't know *what* is true yet," said the Badger severely.

Beryl looked from face to face. "What? *What* is true, or possibly not?"

But the Badger said no more, only handed the newspaper to her. It had been folded back to an article upon the front page. She glanced at the headlines.

NOTORIOUS TOAD ON THE RAMPAGE!
Valuable Motor-cycles Destroyed, Stolen
Young Rabbit Kidnapped by Vile Amphibian
"They could be anywhere," says Scotland Yard

There was a photograph beneath the headline, rather blurry, of a motorcycle on a Town street. The camera-shot was from behind, but visible as riders were a portly (not to say obese) figure in a leather riding suit, and a slender form that Beryl recognized immediately by its gown and bonnet as the Rabbit. She looked up at the others with concern.

"Read on, Miss Mole," said the Badger grimly. "I had this newspaper from one of the Stoats in the Wild Wood, who thought I might want to read about 'our friend the Toad.' Paugh! I clouted him for his effrontery, but—well, you'll see. It is sensational—it is overwrought—but there may be some germs of truth in it."

Beryl skimmed the article quickly. It was long and breathless in tone, for this was not a sensible, sedate newspaper of the sort that dealt with dry matters of State and Government; this was the most sensational sort of journalism, bright as the sun and yellow as buttercups. A dangerous felon (the Toad) had brutally terrorized the hapless proprietor of a reputable shop, as well as his shop-men, a mechanic, a respectable nurse, and a worthy widow (that was Madame Celeste, in private life the relict of one Jeronimo Thomas Webb), to say nothing of scores of passersby. The Toad had wantonly destroyed a valuable racing motor-cycle and an expensive glass window and threatened (with a laugh) to toss a frightened infant into a rubbish-bin. An innocent Rabbit chancing to walk past at that moment identified him as the notorious Toad, at which he seized her, hurled her onto a nearby motor-cycle, and rode away, with her screaming in terror. Courageous constables had attempted to stop him, but it was all for naught: he fled through the Town, demonstrating a complete disregard for bystanders and vehicular ordinances (this part at least was true), and they had lost him. He was assumed to be hiding out in a secret lair somewhere in the Home Counties, and should be considered extremely dangerous. Important clergymen had been asked to pray for the well-being and safe release of the unknown, unfortunate Rabbit. (There was no mention of the money Toad had cast behind him as he rode away; it had been silently agreed by all present that its appearance was more in the way of an accident than a payment, and the earliest stage of the pursuit had been impaired by dozens of people scrambling about after the guineas rolling about, and the bank notes fluttering everywhere.)

A casual reader might be forgiven for assuming that the Toad was a sort of cross between Black Bart and Dr Crippen, but even setting aside the story's obvious hyperbole, things looked quite bad for the Toad. Beryl said, "I cannot believe that Lottie would encourage any of this—this *errant* behavior of the Toad's!"

"He did not take her hostage, anyway," said the Badger.

Beryl sighed. "No, I am sure she is quite willingly part of whatever is going on, even if she didn't initiate it. This is going to be just like the bank-robbery misadventure, all over again."

"Perhaps they planned this between them," said the Water Rat.

"I don't think so," said Beryl. "Lottie is not an *organized* individual, and it doesn't seem to me as though the Toad is that sort, either."

The Water Rat asked, "Well then, where are they now? Toad can't come back here; everyone will be looking for him. And he can't go anywhere else—he'll be identified, and that will be the end of him. He will have to flee to the Continent,

I suppose—except that they'll be looking for him there, *and* at all the aerodromes and ports. What an *ass* that Toad is! I know, Badger"—for the Badger was looking reproachfully at him—"I am worried for him, of course, and Miss Rabbit, as well; but to do something so foolish, right in the middle of the summer. Our busiest time of year! It's too much, it really is. I don't mean to crab, because things are as bad as they can be, but still, there you are."

Everyone nodded. There, indeed, they were.

In near silence Beryl offered elevenses to everyone; in near silence they assented; in near silence they all sat at the little table beneath the chestnut tree, munching seedcake and thinking. Every so often, one or another of them said, "What if we ——," and the rest all replied, "No, no, that won't work, because ——."

The cake was gone and the Mole was glumly lowering the empty plate to the grass for the ants when Beryl cried suddenly. "O, I have it!"

"What?" said three voices.

She said, "The Hills! I wonder I did not think of it before this! It is where she and I are from. No one in the news article knows who *she* is—they said the *unknown* Rabbit; did you mark it?—so no one will look for *her*, and they shall not be looking for Mr Toad in that direction, either. If Mr Toad and Lottie can but *get* there, they may *lie low* (as I think the phrase is) until this mess can be sorted out."

The Mole had said nothing to this point, but now (though he was usually the most amiable fellow imaginable) he said indignantly, "Of course Toad *would* do that, head to the Hills and make things hot for a lot of perfectly respectable folks who don't even know him. It's bad enough he does this to us—we're used to him! But to bother the Rabbit's family and, and everyone else there—"

The Badger said grimly, "Peace, Mole. I'll make things hotter still for him when he finally returns to the River Bank."

"*If* we can get him back here," interjected the Water Rat.

Beryl was not paying attention. "So long as there is no further news in this wretched rag, we may assume Toad has not been apprehended, and all is well—as well as it can be, anyway. Badger, will you ask this Stoat if he will lend you the newspaper each day?"

The Badger nodded. "I will, though I can tell you that it goes against the grain to ask *anything* of a Stoat."

She nodded. "And I shall write to Lottie's mother— indeed, I must, to tell her what has happened!—and I will ask her to tell us when—if—they arrive. I don't know how I can explain my neglect, though! I promised to watch over her, and now this."

"It is like trying to look after a small hurricane," said the Mole tartly. "*All* Rabbits are like that. I don't see how any self-respecting Mole could think it was possible."

"Rabbits are flighty," agreed Beryl, but said no more.

They were worried for their friends, but they were also animals (even if charmingly dressed, property-owning animals), and it is not the way of animals to worry for long. An animal lives in the long *now* of the world. Her life is good or bad in the moment: she starves or feasts, freezes or warms herself, trembles or rejoices; and then that moment is gone. She blinks and shakes herself and moves into a newer *now*, each in its turn.

Beryl, the Mole, and the others could do nothing for their friends but wait. But mooning about, waiting to hear the worst, biting their paws and tying their handkerchiefs into knots—this was not the animals' way, and O, it was water-lily season, and impossible to stay long off the water. And so, when the last of the tea had been drunk (and unless you have tried it, you have no idea how pleasant tea can be on a hot day, after it has cooled in porcelain cups for a while), the Water Rat said, "I think I will go out for a row, down to the weir and back. Would anyone care to join me?"

But the Badger shook his head and rose ponderously. "No, Rat. I have things to do, and Toad has already lost me half the day. I'll return home and speak with the Stoat about the newspaper." He bowed to Beryl and was gone.

Beryl also shook her head, regretfully. "No, I must write to Lottie's mother before anything else—but I so wish I could, Rat! I have always wished to row on the water. How kind of you to invite me."

"You've never been on the water?" the Rat said in astonishment.

She shook her head as she cleared their dishes (though she did not see the cake plate, and it sat in the grass until the next day) onto a tray. "Is it pleasant?"

"Well, that doesn't seem right at all! We could always wait a few minutes, couldn't we, Moley?" said the Water Rat good-naturedly.

"Would you?" Beryl said, brightening. "I shall be quick, then." She carried the tray inside, and in a moment, the Water Rat and the Mole could see her seating herself at a desk just inside one of the Cottage's windows, to write the promised letter.

The Water Rat turned to the Mole with a laugh. "That means we have just time for a pipe before she returns. Imagine having lived here all these weeks and not having rowed yet! Still, I suppose females don't have the same opportunities."

"Ratty," said the Mole, "I'm afraid I shan't go with you."

"What?" said the Water Rat. "Not . . . go . . . rowing! Aren't you feeling well, Moley? You can't allow this business with Toad to upset you. It's not our way, we animals, to be miserable if we can help it. There's enough reasons in the general run of things without looking for trouble."

The Mole said, "It's not that—or not very much. O, I can't help but feel bad for Toad. He could be lost or injured, or in gaol already—or worse! And us, knowing nothing of it before tomorrow's newspapers. No, it's *her*. I can't and won't go out onto the water with Beryl."

"Miss Mole? I wish you'd said something, old chap; you know, if I had to choose, I would much rather be out with you than her—practically a stranger, and a female too, you know." His expression sharpened. "What is it about you two? You avoid her, and when you can't avoid her, you say nothing at all; and when you *must* say something, you are as near to rude as I have seen you with anybody, ever. You have spent hardly any time with her, so *why* do you dislike her so? I know, we all thought she should spoil things, but she hasn't, has she? And it's not fair to blame her for the Rabbit."

The Mole said in a low voice, "I knew her—before. Before I met you, before I came to Mole End. She was part of why I left my first home and came to Mole End."

The Water Rat exclaimed, "Why, Mole! Why have you never mentioned this?"

"There were reasons," he said wretchedly, but before he could add anything, Beryl was running back down the lawn, with a parasol and a little basket with a loaf of bread peeking from its top, which boded well for the enterprise.

She said as she approached, "Done! And sent off with the Mouse to be posted immediately." (The Mouse was the maid.) "Gentlemen, I am ready if you are."

"We shall be soon enough," said the Water Rat. "Moley—" He turned, but the Mole had slipped away already, silently and without a word. He said awkwardly, "Well—Mole cannot join us, sadly—things to do, you know—a very busy chap, old Mole."

He worried that Beryl might be hurt by the sudden decampment, but she said nothing about it, only smiled secretly and said to the Water Rat, "Then it will be that much more food for the two of us! I put in the last of the seedcake, and some potted meat and a nice Dutch cheese and some bread and mustard, and— If that is all right?"

And her expression was so happy and hopeful that the Water Rat could no more say No to her than he could to the sun as it strolled across the sky, or the moon's steady changes. He grinned at her. "I only need a moment to ready the boat. There is a little dock at the foot of the lawn, down among the rushes. Do you know it?"

Beryl nodded eagerly.

"Then I shall scull up and pick you up in ten minutes," he promised.

It was more than ten minutes, for the Water Rat had to clean up his boat a bit—as a bachelor, he did not always keep things quite as neat as a lady might like, and then there were a few boat cushions to be wiped clean and tossed into the bow for her comfort—but it was still less than twenty before he tied the painter to the cottage dock. Beryl was waiting, and quickly handed down the basket—it was satisfyingly heavy—and her parasol, and then hopped down into the boat herself, causing it to rock a bit before she settled herself into the bow.

"Where to?" asked the Water Rat amiably.

"Just the other day I was up the River—upon a bicycle," she explained. "So down, perhaps? To the weir, you said? Or will rowing back be too much labor?"

"Labor!" said the Water Rat as he dug in with the oars and took them into the current. "No, indeed. We are only going out for an hour or two, after all—hardly time to tire ourselves out. A nice row back in the coolness of the evening—why, it will be just what we need after we empty that basket of yours!"

O, the River! The Water Rat sculled them across to the other bank and they dawdled their way downstream from there, peering into every inlet and lagoon. They chatted a bit in soft voices of this and that, but Beryl had the rare gift of silence, and much more of the time they said nothing.

The Water Rat was not to know that the silences were not hers to control. She had completed the morning's labors, but the Novel was still talking to her, endlessly, demanding she notice the osiers, their smell, like . . . wood, or reeds perhaps, or even (if it could be phrased properly) nothing but themselves. The ducks, dabbling in a little backwater, tails up, bright yellow legs paddling the air: charming and easy to describe, but to what end? And there was a willow, bowed down so far that when she and the Water Rat floated through its drooping wands, they found themselves in a shimmering chapel made of long silver leaves that whispered in the tiny breeze. Could this be used in some fashion?

And there was the River itself: the changing, dancing water . . . the reflection of sunlight that now concealed, now revealed the duckweed that waved below the surface . . . a trout, shining with a thousand rainbows, suspended as though in crystal, until it flicked its tail and was gone into the shadow of the bank . . . the sound of the water against the boat's hull, like the bars of a rosewood xylophone brushed with a velvet mallet: *chook*, *chingle*; a sweet, rippling, chiming sound— But no, there were no words. The Novel and the River confronted one another in Beryl; and, this time, in this manner, the River triumphed in that it permitted no words for itself; and the Novel acknowledged defeat, and let Beryl be for a while.

Down Beryl and the Water Rat floated until they came at last to a place where the River divided itself to pass on either side of a small, tangled island; and weirs stretched across both branches, wood and wire and a rippling of the water the only signs of where they were, from upstream.

"There," said Beryl. "The island between the weirs. Let's stop there for a little."

"If you think so," said the Water Rat.

She heard a certain wariness in his tone. "Do you think it is dangerous to stop so close to the weirs?"

"If you mean, can I row us away when we are done, of course I can," said the Water Rat, a bit crossly, then added, more thoughtfully, "It's not the weirs. But the island . . . We animals don't go here, that's all. It's dangerous. It is, but I can't tell you how, exactly. Not dangerous to your life, but . . . something else. Why can't I remember? Otter—you know Otter? His son Portly got lost there—last year it was. We found him but. . . . It's so quiet, you see," he finished lamely.

"So are we quiet," said Beryl. "There—that little inlet. It will be all right, I think. And even if it's not— Rat, I feel as though I *must* go here, no matter what happens. Can you understand that?"

And he could, though he could not remember why. Silently he rowed them into the inlet, which was narrow as a stream, hung over by rushes bent nearly to the water. She knelt in the bow and pushed them aside with her paws as they advanced; but it was only a few yards before the water opened out into a little lagoon bounded with waist-high reeds, trees towering to meet overhead so that the sunlight came through in patches. The water was hidden by the green disks and white wheels of lilies, so many lilies, laid over and across one another until the water showed only in tiny black scraps. The space was utterly still except for flecks of buzzing light that were insects hovering above the lilies, caught for a moment in the shafts of sunlight. The Water Rat raised his oars, and they glided silently until they came to rest amid the water lilies. Beryl leaned over the boat's side and touched them, one by one. She plucked one, and it came free with a little splash. Its long, bright green stem and white petals glowed against her dark skirt. At its heart was a cluster of yellow stamens. A single dragonfly, red as enamel, had been resting upon it; it lifted and vanished in a soundless movement, a curving line across the air that shone for a moment in their eyes.

On one side was a little grassy bank that came down to the very edge of the lagoon; they could see the short grass went under the water a little way, as though the water was not always this high. Wordlessly, the Water Rat grounded his boat upon the bank, and Beryl stepped out in a daze, unmindful of the water that came to her ankles.

"I can't leave the boat," said the Water Rat, and his simple voice was softened, muted by the lilies and their pads. "There is nothing to tie it to."

Beryl nodded. "I shan't be a moment," she said, as though this were the most normal thing anyone could do, walk alone and without explanation into the little wilderness that rose all around them. She stepped up the bank to a clump of loosestrife and passed beyond it. For a moment, he could still see the white lily in her paw against the shady undergrowth, and then that, too, was lost to the Water Rat's sight.

The Water Rat waited in the still lagoon and looked at the lilies. The air was still and sleepy. He loved water lilies as he loved everything about the River, though they were laborious to scull through and usually there was no point to doing so, for lilies collected in still places, dead ends, places that led from nowhere to nowhere. The pads were not quite perfect circles, each a tiny field with a slim green fence; and the lilies rose among them like trees: opened, half-opened, and buds. The Rat was a poet and had once tried to write a poem about them. He had compared the lilies to stars in the sky, and rhymed *white* with *light* and *sprite*; but the words had dried on his pen, and he had set that poem aside in a cubbyhole of his desk and never returned to it. But he could still look on them with pleasure, and so he did so, and waited dreamily.

And after a time, Beryl returned. There was a quickness to her steps now, and her eyes were bright. The lily that had been in her hands was gone. "Rat!" she said, and her voice was light and sweet, very unlike her normal low, calm tones. "O, I have seen Him!"

The Water Rat straightened; had he been napping? "Seen who?" he said, ungrammatically.

"Him! O, Rat, you did not say that He was here! Can you hear them? Even now—His pipes—there, listen! . . . You are right, O, He is dangerous, yes—but not to us animals, surely not." Her eyes shone. "He spoke to me, and I worshipped at His feet. Have not you?"

It came to the Rat for one perfect instant, the memory, full and complete and free of loss or regret, of that blessed night last summer when he and the Mole had walked across the Island and seen Him, the Protector of Small Animals: His kind, wild eyes and human face; the wooden pipes in His long brown fingers; the curved horns that sprang from His forehead; His goat's-legs, fine and strong and glossy brown; and little Portly the Otter between His hooves, asleep within earshot of the deadly weir.

"Yes," said the Water Rat. "Yes!" and it all made sense in that instant, for writing was a sort of divine madness, and who better to see the God of divine madness than one who wrote? He, the Water Rat, was a poet, and he knew he saw more than dear Mole or the Badger or the Otter—or Toad, bless his heart!—but Beryl, he knew now, was one of His own, adopted child of the god, never to be free of His regard. She would never have a day that she did not see something and hear a voice in her mind say, *Remember this and then write this.*

And he realized suddenly that he had no wish to take on that burden. He could write, or not write. Days or weeks could pass by without him setting pen to paper, or even thinking of poetry. *He*, if he chose, could mess about with rhymes as someone else might with boats: a passion, but one that could be set aside or ignored.

As though he had closed a book, the memory slipped away. "Miss Mole," he said kindly, for she was staring into the air as though listening to something; but the space around the lilies was silent, quite silent. "Beryl, come into the boat."

And she did. They said little on the long row back. It was hard, in spite of the Water Rat's words earlier, but he welcomed the labor. The day was nearly faded—how had they spent so much time on the River? But they had not started in the morning; that must be it—and gnats rose up in clouds that stained the air. Beryl said aloud, "I shall have to rewrite most of it; I see the problem now." He knew she was not speaking to him and said nothing.

It was nearly dark when he let her off at last at the Cottage's dock, and she smiled down at him in the dimming light: "Thank you, Rat, for a lovely day."

"Thank you, Miss Mole," he replied, and after a moment's pause he considered his next words. "May I ask—?"

But she was gone already, running up the lawn to the cottage, to the Novel and the changes that had become so clear to her on the island between the weirs.

It was downstream from her cottage to his own comfortable hole, so he floated down, content to be the Water Rat, to have spent the day with his River. But those lilies, now—they really were worth writing about. When he got home, he might dig out that old poem and try again. Or perhaps not—for as he approached the bank by his hole, the Mole was waiting for him and ran down to catch the painter and tie the boat up.

"Was it a good day?" said the Mole shyly, as the Water Rat handed up the cushions. "I want to apologize for being so surly! I should have gone."

"Well, as to that," began the Water Rat, and then stopped. In the bow was Beryl's little basket. "Why, we forgot all about the seedcake and sandwiches! Where *did* the time go?"

Chapter Seven
Flight

When the Toad came back to his senses in the bramble beside the signpost, he could not at first recollect what exactly had happened. There had been a delightful sensation of speed and the wind in his face, almost as though he had been flying; the great vibrating roar of some magnificent machine in his proximity; and a great complacency, a sense that, among all those who walked upon the face of the Earth, he was the finest. "So at least I remember who I am, even if I don't know anything else!" he said to himself: "Toad of Toad Hall! Why, it's a pleasure to recollect I am Toad, and not some other poor wretch—old Badger, for instance, admirable chap though he is!"

He was unaware he had spoken aloud, but—"Of course you're the Toad!" said a voice not his own, a young female voice quivering with what sounded like relief. "O thank goodness, you are coming back to yourself!"

Though his eyes were still closed, he became aware of his surroundings: He was in some outdoor venue (he could hear insects and bird song, and a barking dog a short way off), lying upon his back across a root or something uncomfortable, amid something else that was pricking him all over his exposed flesh, his paws and feet and face; and he was very uncomfortable. And what voice was this? Someone was chafing one of his paws. He opened one eye.

It was the Rabbit! She had cast her bonnet aside and, heedless of the blackberry brambles tearing her ribbons and the ripe berries staining her skirts, she knelt over him, ears twitching with concern, his limp paw between hers. It all came flooding back to him—the motor-cycle—the police—the chase through Town—the flight across the countryside—the final crack-up—his unhappy situation. Tears began to flow. "O no!" he wailed. "Doomed—doomed!"

The Rabbit said anxiously, "I don't think your injuries are *that* bad, dear Toad! No broken bones—no parts missing—your skull uncracked . . . You have a few scratches and bruises, but it *is* fortunate that we fell into these brambles, or things should have been much worse, you know. Indeed, we are quite lucky!"

But the Toad could not be comforted. "Doomed," he wailed. Enormous tears rolled from his eyes to puddle in his ears. "O, I am such a vain, foolish Toad! *What* was I thinking? My home, my friends, my wealth—Lost! Torn away! Gone, because I could—not—restrain—myself!" He sat up, but could hardly hold his head upright for his gusty weeping. "Ratty—Mole—Otter—dear old Badger—they all warned me, again and again—told me that I must learn to be a better Toad—but I did not listen—and now I'm for it! No hope, no hope at all!" He threw himself down again full-length among the brambles (though avoiding the worst of them) and absolutely let himself go.

The Toad's display of sorrow—long, noisy, and damp— was not for the faint of heart, but the Rabbit had many younger siblings and she had seen worse—though, to be just, never before from anyone grown to adulthood. She looked around, but there was no vase convenient, that she might dash its contents into the Toad's face and break his hysterical frenzy. Nor did she think she could bring herself to slap him—someone of the male persuasion, and very nearly a stranger! But her reticule had somehow remained on her wrist through the long activity-filled day, and she pulled from it a little bottle of smelling salts, uncapped it, and waved it beneath his broad nostrils.

"O!" said the Toad, arrested in mid-wail, choking at the strong smell. "What are you doing, you detestable female?"

"Trying to calm you!" said the Rabbit, a little tartly, for her day had not been one of unalloyed delight, either. "And I am *not* detestable."

"No, you're not," acknowledged the Toad with a flush of shame. "I know that; it is only my own selfishness speaking. You . . . mean well, I know that. . . . If you are brutal, it is . . . not intentional. . . . But my constitution is more delicate that one would think, to look at me."

"I am sure not!" said the Rabbit robustly. "Why, you are— hsst! Listen!"

They heard the clop of hooves and the creaking of wheels: a horse and cart approaching. It came to a stop as the Toad and the Rabbit stared at one another with wide eyes. Someone got down from the cart, and then a second person, and then there were footsteps closer, closer. . . .

"Hullo!" said a voice just outside the bramble: a female, country voice. "Look, Ned—here's a ruined motor-cycle! Someone's taken a spill!"

A second voice—male; this must be Ned—exclaimed, "Right you are, Mum!" and called, "Hullo? Is anyone in there?"

The terror-stricken Toad said nothing, only cowered in his place, but the Rabbit cried out, "Yes, O yes! We have been in a terrible accident. Please help us!"

"No!" With a scream, Toad leapt to his feet, and collapsed instantly into a deep swoon.

When the Toad at last returned (again) to consciousness, he found himself tucked into a soft bed between sheets that smelled deliciously of lavender; and since in his experience dungeons were not generally furnished with such amenities, he sat up cautiously and looked about himself. There was a cheery fire in a grate, burned down now but still bright enough that he could see the room he was in: a small, cheerful space with sloping ceilings and a dormer window with curtains pulled cozily against the night he could see peeping through a gap. There was a rocking chair turned to face the fire so that its back was to him, and a red quilt upon his bed. He could smell that someone had put arnica on his bruises, and a bulky white bandage was wrapped tightly around his head, which made him look (though he did not know it) a bit like the evil genie in a fairy story. There was a pitcher of cool water and a cup upon the bedside table; he drank thirstily.

"Not so bad, not so bad," he said to himself complacently. "Another narrow escape, it looks like. I wonder if I can get a splash of brandy brought up to me?" And he started to look around for a bell-pull.

The rocking chair shifted suddenly, and someone unfolded herself and crossed the room to his side to peer nearsightedly at him. It was a very old woman, with a face the approximate shape, color, and texture of a withered turnip, scattered with dark spots. "There, there, young sir," she said, and he recognized her voice as the one he had heard outside the brambles, "lie still, lie still. You took a narsty spill, you did. Narsty. If me and my boy Ned hadn't found ye, there's no telling how things might have ended, but no harm done, no harm. How are you feeling, now?"

"Not well," wheezed the Toad feebly. "Brandy . . ."

The old lady laid a hand on Toad's forehead. "Brandy! Brandy's no good for tumbles, no good at all. No fever, that's good. Nah, you lie back now and don't worry yourself. We brought you back, along o' whatever bits of that motor-cycle were big enough to pick up off the ground, but I'm sad to tell you that it's ruined completely, says my Ned, and he knows what's what, about machines and engines and such-like."

The Toad cast one paw over his eyes with a groan. "The Dustley!"

"I daresay, I daresay. And your sister—aow, I know you'll be that worr—"

"My sister?" said the Toad weakly. "O! My sister. Yes."

"No, no need to worry about her, sir! She's fine—hardly a scratch. Very nimble she must a' been, too, a-flying off the back of that motor-cycle when you cracked up, not to hit something. A very nice young animal, she is, and you should be proud of her: polite, and not above helping an old woman upstairs with t' hot water. You just lie still, now—the doctor'll be along a' here in a moment."

The Toad lay back with a sigh. "A doctor! The very thing—"

Back at the River Bank, the Toad had liked doctors; in fact, they had become rather a hobby of his in recent years, whenever nothing better was going on and his friends were busy. He summoned them often, especially on drab, rainy days in the autumn. Phantom pains, ominous coughs, strange sneezes, possible skin-splotches, an itch or a watery eye or a worrisome ear: anything was reason enough. The village doctor had not lasted past his first visit, when he had suggested that the Toad's problems might be rooted, not in some mysterious ailment but in his corpulence and idle habit of life; but once the sufferer began to bring in eminent practitioners from Town, he found them very helpful indeed. He was listened to with courteous attention as he described his symptoms, again and again, in ever-greater detail. The doctors shook their heads gloomily and remarked upon his stoic courage, and recommended consultations with specialists (generally acquaintances planning costly trips to Egypt or the Holy Land), and suggested follow-up visits, on the expectations of which they ordered expensive new motor-cars for their wives. Syrups were concocted and tablets compounded; plasters applied and liniments prescribed. The Toad listened meekly and took such advice and medicines as did not run counter to his own preferences, and since his pains and ailments always vanished as soon as something interesting happened again—a boating expedition with the Water Rat, for instance, or a sunny day suitable for lawn bowling—it can be seen that this was an innocent, wholesome amusement, harming no one and profitable, in its way, to all.

So, for slightly fewer than ten seconds, the Toad looked forward to the arrival of this doctor. He closed his eyes and began cataloguing what he could feel: neck—stiff; right paw—bruised; foot—itchy. And then it came to him: with doctors came questions, questions that might (no—*would*) be awkward to answer. Why, they should find out about the motor-cycle and the accident and the chase and— He opened his eyes wide and cried, "No! No doctors!" and swung his legs from the bed.

But the old lady shook her head and inexorably returned his legs to their original position. "Nah, nah, it's for t' best. No gentleman wants to see a doctor, I know, but we wouldn't want you to die in our wee house, me and Ned, and 'Better safe than sorry' is our motto, it is. And I'll be honest with you, young sir: I don't like your color, I don't. Our old doctor'll set you up finely."

"Unnecessary," croaked the Toad, feeling panic well up. "I feel entirely well! In fact—"

He would have said more, but at that moment the door to the room opened a crack and the Rabbit peeped in. She said, "I thought I heard voices, and—O! I am so happy to see you awake, T—dear brother!" She tripped up to the side of the bed and, after a pause, kissed his bandaged forehead in a sisterly fashion.

"Mmm," said the poor Toad. It had been a very long day, beginning with the train into Town and ending with quite a substantial tumble into a blackberry bramble, and things were moving along a bit quickly for his lagging mind.

The old woman was looking down at them dotingly. "Isn't that the sweetest thing?" she said. "She was that worried about you, your sister. Now that you're awake and your sister's right here, I'll just pop downstairs and make a posset or two. The doctor'll be here in two shakes of a lamb's tail, he will, and then you'll be just as right as rain."

The Rabbit had barely waited for the door to shut behind the old woman's retreating figure before she said, "Toad, how exciting! Why, we are criminals!"

"I must flee!" The Toad flung aside his bedclothes. He was most conveniently still garbed in his motor-cycle riding suit, as removing over-tight leathers from an unconscious, obese Toad had proved to be beyond the skills of the old woman (and she had not quite liked to in any case, thinking it a liberty); and so she had left them on, taking only his overcoat and helmet. "Did you hear her, Rabbit? Doctors! And right after doctors come constables—and then it shall be Scotland Yard and the Tower! Alas!"

"Surely not!" said the Rabbit. "I don't think the doctor can have heard anything about what happened in Town."

"You think!" cried the Toad, trembling in every limb. "Even now, the news of our activities is being flashed by wire across the country! Telegrams! Telegraphs! Couriers on motor-cycles even faster than the Nonpareil! The evening papers—full of it! Pamphlets, I shouldn't wonder—bills upon every wall! Dungeons! Torture! The guillotine! Help me find my coat," he said in quite another tone, one of grim desperation. "I am leaving immediately."

"You can't, Toad! You must stay quiet until the doctor has been here." But she amiably hunted around the room with him, and it was she that found it, folded neatly upon the rush seat of the rocking chair. "Why, the old dear has been mending it! See, here—a bramble tear, sewn up neat as—"

He snatched it away, and searched the pockets. "My money—my guineas, my bank notes! Where have they gone?"

"You threw them behind you as we left the motor-cycle shop," she reminded him helpfully.

"I did?" He stared at her with starting eyes. "I did! All those beautiful bank notes—gone! Tossed to the winds! And for what? Nothing! The motor-cycle is ruined anyway! What a stupid, idiotic, *foolish* thing to do! Penniless—bereft—on the lam! Can't go home! No money to go elsewhere! What—can—I—do?" Sobbing, he threw himself down again on the bed, evidently preparing for a weeping fit which bade fair to throw all the day's prior fits into the shade.

The Rabbit said hastily, "Wait! I have a bit of money, I think." Her reticule was still about her wrist, and now she dumped its contents out onto the red coverlet. "I have . . . three, four, or—here's another shilling, and one, two, three sixpences, and O! A pound note—" After a moment, she lifted her head with a delighted expression. "Why, Toad, I have quite a surprising amount! I recall now—my quarterly allowance came only last week, and I have spent almost none of it yet." She began stuffing the money back into the reticule.

The Toad, face down in a pillow and still teetering on the brink of his incipient fit, moaned, "Money? Pennies and pounds! What *good* will it do us? We are doomed, quite doomed! Fugitives! Nowhere to go—nowhere to hide—they will be looking for us everywhere!"

The Rabbit wrinkled her brow. "Well, we *could* go to my relatives. In fact, what a grand idea! I am not expected home for visit before Christmas-time—everyone will be so happy to see me! It shall be such a surprise to them! Mummy and Daddy and all my little brothers and sisters, and my aunties and—and you shall be my guest, so *that's* all right. Toad, it will be a great adventure!"

The Toad lifted his head from the pillow and eyed her. "Where do they live?"

"Why, the Hills!"

That had an unpleasantly rustic sound. "*Which* hills?" he asked.

"*The* Hills, of course! They are some distance from here, to the north and west. That way, I think." She pointed at a black-and-white lithograph of *The Monarch of the Glen* upon one wall. "Or perhaps not. I am a little turned around, you know."

The Toad rolled upright and mopped tentatively at his cheeks. "Can you find the way from here, do you think?"

"O, I would imagine so. I was with Beryl before, who is ever so much better with maps and train schedules and things, but—I mean, they're *hills*! They're large, so all we need do is look about a little. It should not be diffi—"

They heard a door downstairs open and slam shut, and voices—several voices. "It is the doctor!" squealed the Toad.

"O, good!" said the Rabbit, "Now we may have you looked at, and then make our—"

But the Toad wasted no more time on fruitless speech. He rushed to the dormer, hopped onto the window-seat, threw open the casement, and looked out. It was a second-story window but it led conveniently onto a low sloped roof (the kitchen, had they known it). It was the work of an instant for him to heave himself over the sill and onto the roof. With a great clattering, he galloped across the tiles to a tree at the opposite end (it was a pear tree, quite overgrown), and threw himself into its thick branches. He did not shin so much as cascade down its trunk in a shower of leaves, small branches, and spiders and half-ripe pears; and landed upon all fours in a garden that smelled of wet dirt and carrots. Wasting not a moment, he galloped to the bottom of the garden, through a withy fence (fumbling the gate's latch in his haste), and onto a small lane. He cast agonized glances to the left and right, but he was unobserved. Safe! No—there were light footsteps coming down the garden. Where to go, where to go? He sobbed aloud in terror.

"Why, Toad!" said the Rabbit. She clipped the gate shut neatly behind them and stood beside him. "How fortuitous—a lane!" she said admiringly. "And just where we needed it, too. Which way shall we go? I brought your coat," she added, and gave it to him.

Rabbit—the Hills—her relatives—her reticule. "Excellent Rabbit, admirable Rabbit," said the Toad humbly. "We shall go wherever you say."

The Rabbit led the Toad left along the lane until it debouched into another, slightly larger road, and turned left again. The moon was not yet up, but the eastern sky glowed with dim silver light, veiling the stars: it was this light the Rabbit was using to direct them. They walked a long time in silence, the Toad straining his every cell listening for pursuit, and the Rabbit, apparently, perfectly content with their midnight promenade. The moon at last shook free of the horizon and began to shine behind them, making long, deeply black shadows: a tall, infinitely slender Rabbit with ears that stretched yards ahead of them, and a rounder, less defined shape that was the Toad, thinned and stretched nearly to normal proportions. Each step took them into their own shadows, but always the shadows moved forward, as well. They saw few others: an Owl that swept past overhead but did not pause; a large party of bats dancing (noisily, thought the Rabbit, but the Toad heard nothing) just beyond the circle of light cast by a lantern outside a country tavern door; a Hedgehog and her family on their way home from a late visit to her sister's. They avoided villages where people might be found.

The moon was halfway to the zenith when the Toad at last gave up. He had been about to ask the Rabbit whether they might stop for a little, when they came to a Fox, leaning upon a stone wall and smoking a pipe in the darkness—"Onion sauce!" he jeered; "Garlic and butter!"—but he had dined already and otherwise he left them alone. Still, for a while after that, neither wanted to stop. But at last the Toad had had enough, which he evidenced by throwing himself down into the dirt in the middle of the country lane and refusing to go farther. He wailed (but softly, still mindful of the Fox), "I can't go on—I can't!" and it was the Rabbit who found a little corncrib that they climbed into. They spent the rest of the night there, and the Toad slept surprisingly well, though he woke up thirsty and ready for breakfast.

Sadly, breakfast was not forthcoming—or at least there was nothing he would consider *true* breakfast: no soft-boiled eggs and rashers of bacon and kippers and toast and marmalade and jam and fresh butter and coffee and—well, it didn't bear thinking about; but the Toad *did* think about it and couldn't stop, even after they came to an orchard and filled the Rabbit's kerchief with apples, and even after the Rabbit boldly went into a village and bought bread and cheese for them. She brought back as well a copy of a newspaper from Town (in fact, the same that Badger had been given by the Stoat, back in the Wild Wood), and they read it to one another as they ate their breakfast on a village common clustered with amiable but uninterested cows. The Toad had been in rather a subdued mood throughout the long night, but being called "dangerous," "reprehensible," and "blackguardly" in a single paragraph brought him into something more nearly approaching his normal bumptious state; and as the days passed and no one apprehended them, his glee grew.

They travelled on foot, or by cadging such rides as they could find, which ranged from the backseat of a vast and impressive motor-car—they explained that they were on their way to Portsmouth to attend the deathbed of an agèd relative, and were treated with great kindness and head-pattings—to the tail of an oxcart, which lasted until the driver saw them and threatened them with his goad. They travelled north and west, as the Rabbit had suggested, and by the middle of the first afternoon, when they saw the distant blue shapes of hills against the sky, nearly faded into the thick summertime air, they were both satisfied that this was the correct direction.

Every morning and evening there were newspapers filled with headlines in 48-point type (or even larger): VILLAINOUS TOAD STILL AT LARGE! SCOTLAND YARD BAFFLED; but no one seemed to associate *this* Toad and Rabbit with *that* Toad and Rabbit; or perhaps the excitements of urban crime simply mattered less out here.

For once, the Toad regretted his notoriety. It came hard on a creature whose general practice when travelling was to strut up to proprietors saying, "Do you know who I am?" and then order the best chambers and meals; harder still, because he was a deeply hospitable creature and it went sorely against his nature for the Rabbit to pay for everything at the more modest hostelleries they frequented. If innkeepers looked askance at an unaccompanied female travelling with a male who was clearly no relation—for not everyone was as nearsighted as the kindly old woman who had rescued them, and her Ned (reckoning it was none of his business and rather hoping for a douceur for retrieving the Dustley) had said nothing—well, they stayed silent about it; paying custom was paying custom, after all.

The Rabbit's allowance, however, could not last forever, and now she showed her worth even more concretely. It turned out that she was quite adept at stealing eggs from beneath the hens, scoops of fresh butter from the churns, and, even, once, a ham hanging from the rafters of a cottage. The Toad was less useful, alas: his mood veered wildly between abject despair and unjustified self-confidence. In one moment, he could hardly bring himself to eat more than a morsel of whatever food the Rabbit managed to find for them; in the next, his natural optimism returned and he assumed that all would be well. Grandiose plans that involved stowing aboard an ocean liner and emigrating to America to become a sort of combination railroad magnate and cowboy—"The wide open spaces!" he cried in ecstasy; "Git along o'ye! Twelve points up!"—alternated with visions of drawing and quartering, and of being broken upon the wheel.

The countryside grew rounder and dryer, and there came a point when it was clear that they were at last no longer approaching, but actually *in* the hills.

"Well?" said the Toad. They were standing at a crossroads, and the Rabbit was peering down each road (including the one they had come up) with a flustered expression. He may perhaps be forgiven for his testiness. It was nearly dinner time of the third day, and breakfast, elevenses, luncheon, tea, and "a little bite of something to tide us over 'til dinner" had been sparse, to put it lightly—apples, apples, and more apples— for the countryside had grown less populated, and there had not been so many places where the Rabbit could exercise her acquisitorial skills. This had been puzzling her somewhat, for in her recollection (and she might be a little flighty, as people said, but surely she would not be misremembering after only a few months away?), the Hills were simply *packed* with residents. Indeed, her dear father was always complaining about the crowds and threatening to move away, though nothing ever came of it. A terrible doubt assailed her.

"Do you know, Toad," said she, hesitantly. "I wonder whether these are perhaps not the right hills."

"What?" said the Toad. *"What?"*

Chapter Eight
A Den of Thieves

There are moments when an author must make a choice: whether to present a scene in all the living poetry of its details, or to substitute a paragraph that advances the reader through the narrative in a manner that is economical, succinct, and efficient. The Toad's response to the Rabbit's disclosure offers such a choice to the author—immediacy or concision— but alas! The decision is made for us: our clumsy pen finds itself inadequate to the leisurely challenge of capturing each nuance of Toad's vexation, distress, dejection, wretchedness, and fear: his tearful accusations and sobbing recriminations; his thrashings about and headlong weepings; his first gasp of astonished disbelief and his final gusty sob. The fickle Muse has denied to us her golden touch, and so we instead say merely that the Rabbit's disclosure—and she was quite right; these were *not* the Hills they sought but other, quite different hills—came as an unpleasant shock to the Toad. He wailed and wept, and the Rabbit could only look remorseful and wring her paws, saying, "But indeed, I am not good with directions!"

Still, there came an end to it at last. By now it was dusk, the sky purpling as the shadow of the (wrong) hills rose. The Toad sat in the road with his back against the signpost and his spindly legs stretched out to their full length before him. He was slumped over; and, disheveled, tearstained, and dusty as he was, he might almost have been mistaken for a bundle fallen from the back of a cart, save for the woebegone sniffling he emitted every few seconds, as though he were running on clockwork: a rhythmic counterpoint to the lovely liquid notes of the evening's first tawny-voiced nightingale.

In contrast, the Rabbit stood beside him, still looking very nearly as neat as she had when they left town, if a bit more crumpled. Somehow in their travels, she had found the means of scrubbing the berry stains from her skirt, and she had even been able to sew up the rents where the bramble had torn her gown, for her mother had told her always to carry needle and thread (along with other oddments), and so, most conveniently, they had been in her reticule. But she had lost her hat.

She was a sanguine creature, and it took more than the Toad, even the Toad at his worst, to put her off her stride for long. Long before the end of his fit, she had begun looking about, frowning this way and that, and— "O! I know where we are now!" she said suddenly, well before he had subsided entirely into dejected silence.

A fresh sob burst from the Toad, who added bitterly, "*How* do you know?"

"No, I truly do! Indeed, we are not so far off as we might be. I am just too far north, that is all. Do you see there?" She pointed.

"Yes," he sniffled, not looking.

"My home is just past those trees—that tall clump on the hill, with the single towering oak in their midst," she said happily. "My home, and all my relations, and dear Beryl's family, and the Hares and the dear Dormouses and all our other neighbors, and—and everyone! Home!"

The Toad looked up. She was gazing southward, toward Hills that rose, row after row growing more diffuse until they faded entirely into the purpling dusky sky. Instead of being nearly covered with trees with a few open fields, as *these* hills were, he could see that over there it was all grass and fields, and the trees were mostly limited to the hedgerows.

The Rabbit said, more softly, "Those trees—on the top of the tallest hill—I remember them. My brothers and sisters and I were always running up there to play whenever we could sneak away. It was quite exciting—the seven of us— we would play Pirates, and Highwaymen, and Cavaliers and Roundheads, and—"

"You are sure?" he interrupted, suspicious. "We won't get there and have you say, 'O, I am wrong, it is not *these* trees, it is *those* trees!' will we?"

She continued, unheeding, "—and we said that the tallest tree was the White Tower, and we meant to behead my littlest brother because he was the Pretender, except that Mother found us before we could complete the task. So we never did." She sounded disappointed.

But the Toad was not attending, either: "—because," he said with a quiver in his voice, "if you are wrong—"

But the Rabbit shook herself, and gazed down at him for a moment, and her absent expression reassured him more than anything else might have. "The Hills, Toad! The air is so clear, not at all like the River Bank, where it is so thick; and you can see for miles and miles, and the earth under your toes is light and chalky, not clotty and dark. It has been very interesting, coming to the River Bank with Beryl, and learning to boat, and meeting you all—but— O, the Hills!" She added seriously (and she was seldom serious), "I know they are Home, Toad. I can *feel* it. *You* know."

The Toad was a frivolous creature, but he *did* know— deeply, intimately—the emotion that played across her face. He felt the same way every time he returned to the River Bank after an absence and saw the warm stone walls and shining windows of Toad Hall, the glowing grounds and the stands of trees, each trunk and branch as familiar as his own limbs—and beyond everything, the special, specific shape and sound of the River as it passed just there. *He* knew. It was Home, calling to her. The Rabbit might have been mistaken before this, but no longer.

He brought himself shakily to his feet. He could see the crown of trees she was pointing to, but only as shadows now; the very Hills themselves were already fading into the twilight. "We shall never make it tonight!"

"No," said the Rabbit sadly. "But tomorrow we shall! We must find a place to stay tonight, is all—and quickly, before the Foxes come out."

The Rabbit and the Toad followed the lane that led south from the crossroads as it slipped into a fold of the hills and moved into the shelter of a stand of trees, where night had already collected. There was no good place to walk: there were too many worrisome noises in the hedges that fringed the lane, sudden rustlings and little mocking voices; but when they walked in the middle, they heard an Owl's cruel, low laughter in the branches overhead. The Toad's heart was making what felt like determined attempts to escape through his throat in a trembling scream, but he said nothing as they trotted through the darkness, and even tried to still his breathing: under the circumstances, no easy task for a Toad of nervous disposition but indolent habits. As for the Rabbit, she said nothing but only pulled out the little pocketknife her mother had always advised her to carry in her reticule, and pattered on as quickly as the Toad could move.

The darkness under the trees deepened. The voices in the hedges grew louder, the rustlings closer. The Owl laughed again, and they heard her shake out her feathers, as though preparing to fly. The air ahead of them was a little lighter, and they quickened their pace—even the Toad finding resources he did not know he had.

And then— O blessèd Chance! They were clear of the trees, and they could see around them, and there—just ahead—was the dim shape of a large building in a clearing, and they absolutely *ran* toward it. They saw a dark line where a door was cracked open, and they raced through and slammed it to, just as the Owl on silent wings approached.

They heard her catch herself before she could hit the door, and then her low voice: "Why, dear things! Come out and play!" But they did not, and after another of her cruel laughs, she floated away and was gone.

"What a lucky circumstance!" said the Rabbit, when she could draw breath again. She looked about. They were in a tall dark space, filled with farming implements and piles of hay, with empty box stalls and rooms lining one side, a little two-wheeled whiskey leaning upon its shafts against a wall. "Why, Toad, it's a barn! I have never slept in a barn. It shall be a new adventure for me."

"No more adventures," moaned the Toad despairingly.

"This will perhaps *be* the last adventure before we get to the Hills," she said regretfully. "I don't think much of it, but beggars cannot be choosers, after all. Anyway, there is hay everywhere, so we shall sleep soft at least! And in the morning, off we will go."

Now that the fear of the Owl and the horrid voices in the hedgerows was loosening, the Toad was feeling somewhat better. "I suppose there's no food? No pork-chops, or salads, or *charlottes russes*, or—"

She shook her head. "Unless you can eat oats?" She had lost the last of the apples in their flight.

"*Raw?* Certainly not," he said indignantly, then sighed heavily. "Then I suppose there is nothing to do but sleep."

They crawled up into a haymow that looked down onto the barn's main floor. A Mouse there, seeing they were only a Rabbit and a Toad, said, "You! I was 'ere first. You pipe down an' don't push, a'right?" before returning to sleep.

The Toad wriggled and tossed, and complained that the straw made his skin itch. His nose would *not* stop tickling; he knew, *knew*, he should not be able to sleep for sneezing. But they snuggled in anyway, and while his nose did not stop tickling, he did *not* sneeze (not then, at any rate), and he *did* fall asleep after all, for when the door slid open again, he awoke to find himself sitting stock upright in the straw with a scream trembling upon his lips.

"*Shh!*" hissed the Rabbit. She was awake beside him, on her paws and knees in the straw, peeping down into the main area, where there was a light. The Toad bit back his scream and looked out cautiously, as well.

Someone had brought in a dark lantern and opened it as far as it would go, which was not very far. The dim glow illuminated a wedge of the main floor, leaving everything else in darkness. They could see eight or ten animals: a handful of Stoats and a couple of jostling Weasels, passing around a square dark bottle and gusting with coarse laughter.

"Toad, I think they are criminals!" whispered the Rabbit; she did not sound at all afraid. "But I think they are waiting for something or someone. The Mastermind, perhaps! This is *much* better than merely sleeping in a barn!"

The Toad could not agree, and opened his mouth to say something to her; but alas and alack! The sneeze that had been threatening for so long became manifest, real, and imminent. The Toad scrunched his face and twisted his cheeks, but he could not stop it and it burst from him rather like a sudden shout of thunder from a fast-growing cloud on a hot afternoon. In the dead silence that followed, the Rabbit's voice could be heard saying, "O dear."

In no time at all, two enterprising Stoats found their hiding place in the haymow and dragged Toad and the Rabbit from it (the Mouse had vanished entirely). They were pushed into the lantern's beam, and the Toad fell prostrate onto the main floor. The Rabbit kept her feet and brushed bits of straw from her skirt as she looked into the gloom around them.

"Why—it's a Rabbit!" said a Weasel from the darkness. "And a Toad," said a Stoat from another direction. "A-hiding in our little home!" said a third voice. "Shouldn't you be home, kiddies?" And they all began to cackle in a way the Toad suddenly recognized from the hedgerows they had passed on their way here.

But the Rabbit only shielded her eyes to look into the darkness. "Are you outlaws?" she asked in a voice of great interest. "Is this your hideout?"

"That we are, lassie," said one of the voices, but it did not sound quite so ferocious now. "A band of desprit crim'nals, we are."

"So are *we* criminals, as well!" she exclaimed, but corrected herself, a little sadly: "Well, he is, at any rate. I have only been an aider-and-abetter thus far, but still, it is very exciting."

"Izzat so?" A Weasel stepped forward into the beam of light. Toad raised his head a bit, but the Weasel's expression showed nothing but curiosity. "What sorts a' crime?"

The Toad sat up and opened his mouth, but the Rabbit was before him. "Mostly theft, I believe—isn't that true? Motor-cars and motor-cycles, and horses, and—"

"—and fleeing from the police twice or three times, and prison-break," contributed the Toad, getting to his feet. "And misuse of the public railways, and horse-stealing, and—and this and that. In fact," he ended, and puffed out his chest, "there is very little I *haven't* done!"

During the Toad's speech, the Stoats and Weasels (and a Barn Rat that had thrown in his lot with them) had come closer until they were all clustered in the lantern light in a tight circle, casting long shadows behind them. It was (the Rabbit thought) a *little* bit frightening, but they were more impressed than anything else, nudging one another and whispering, "D'ya 'ear *that?*"—"Escaped the coppers, he did, twice!"—"That's a *proper* outlaw, that is!"; and when he was quite finished (which he did with a little flourish that might almost be a bow), the Barn Rat said, "Three cheers for our friend 'ere!" and handed him the square bottle.

"I don't think—" began the Rabbit. It was too late. The Toad took a drink and immediately burst out choking and coughing, for which he was slapped on the back and cheered; and then a Weasel handed her the bottle, saying, "'Ere you go, lass," and she had to drink as well, and she found that, really, coughing and choking was the only possible response. It tasted—well, it tasted the way she imagined gasoline might, fiery and not at all like the elderflower wine her mother had given her sometimes as a cordial when she was sick—but she managed; and when she looked up with watering eyes, she saw the circle of Stoats and Weasels grinning and cheering her, as well. They seated her upon an upturned pail and started plying the Toad with questions about his exploits. The Toad, I am sorry to say, rather let himself go, and his stories strayed further and further from the unvarnished truth, until their only resemblance to what actually happened was that the Toad featured prominently in both; but the Stoats and Weasels only cheered and asked more questions, and kept the square bottle revolving around the circle.

But even the Toad slowed down after a time, and one of the Weasels turned to the Rabbit, and said, "And what about you, lass?"

"O! I have done nothing, nothing at all," she said. Falling in with bank robbers had been the merest accident, not worth the time it would take to mention, and she did not think they would find the hot-air balloon theft in the least compelling.

The Weasel patted her hand. "Never you mind," he said kindly. "Lasses don't get the same opportunities we gents do, they don't."

"Why, that is what I think!" she said. "And it hardly seems fair."

"But maybe we can put you both in the way of a little something," said the Weasel with a wink. "As soon as the Boss gets 'ere, we'll ask 'im."

"O! So you're here for a reason?" she asked, clasping her paws together in excitement. "Not just to—what do outlaws say—'hang out'?"

A friendly Stoat said, "Right you are, miss! 'Ang out it

is, and why? On account of we got plans to make. And what plans are those? Why, we're planning a great house-robbery, we are! We—"

"WHAT'S ALL THIS?" said a new voice from the darkness outside the lantern's beam: a new voice, smoother and lower-pitched and altogether more frightening. Everyone fell silent instantly and leapt to their feet, looking up a little apprehensively.

Everyone, that is, save the Toad, who had been sitting splay-legged upon the floor in the middle of the circle, thinking deeply. Unlike the Rabbit, he had taken a tot from the bottle each time it passed, and so he was in what is called an exhilarated state—and he took the sudden silence as an opportunity to say: "That's it! Can't go home again—wanted by Scotland Yard—cannot flee the country—it's a life of crime for me, chaps! I've already shown a great appi—an appert—a grape aptitude. Robberies! Holdups! Ban—Banditry! I'll join your gang, fellows!" And he gave the closest approximation to a self-congratulatory bow possible when one is sitting upon a barn floor in an intoxicated condition.

"What's—all—this?" said the smooth voice again, and then a Fox stepped into the light.

A Fox! The Rabbit had seen Foxes before, of course, but never so close: in the Hills, the Rabbits and the Foxes moved in very different circles and did not meet, socially anyway. This Fox was a dapper fellow (in a low way), with a loud tartan waistcoat under his tweedy gameskeeper's coat and not overly clean white gaiters: a slim fellow with ginger hair and bright eyes and an uncomfortable, knowing way about him. He looked down at the nervous circle of Stoats and Weasels and the Barn Rat, and at the Rabbit, and at the Toad, still a-splay and looking, to tell the truth, uncommonly silly.

"Why, boys, we have guests!" he drawled in mock surprise.

His gang had been gazing up at him apprehensively, but he did not seem angry, and they tumbled over one another responding. In the end, one of the Weasels (the one who had patted the Rabbit's hand) piped up. "Aye, Boss, that we do, this 'ere Toad and this 'ere young Rabbit." The Rabbit had come to her feet when the Fox showed up; she dropped a small curtsey. He was taller than she, and swept her a bow that she did not think was truly respectful.

The Weasel—he seemed to be the Head Weasel and the Fox's first lieutenant in crime—continued, "They was a-hiding 'ere when we showed up, but not spying, I don't think. More like 'iding *out*—they says they're crim'nals, same as us. Toad 'ere's a great felon, eight kinds of robbery and jailbreak and who knows what-all; and as for the Rabbit, she's worse'n all o' us put together," and he gave her a little wink that made her blush.

The Fox lifted his brows in faint surprise. "Criminals? *They?* Impossible."

Stories tumbled out of the Stoats and Weasels as they tried to recount the stories they had just heard of the Toad's many misdeeds, real, exaggerated, and entirely fictional. By now the Toad himself had struggled to his feet, and it was he who had the last boastful word when they had finished: "Dirty deebs—*deeds*—of *every* sort."

The Fox stroked his chin thoughtfully. "Hmm. Perhaps we can use you. *And* you, my dear young lady," he said with another mocking bow at the Rabbit, though none of the stories had been of her.

The Head Weasel said, "Right then. The Boss is 'ere, so let's get to work, boys!"

"O, aye!" said all the Stoats and Weasels and the Barn Rat, and everyone sat again. This time the Fox sat with them. There was no sign of the square bottle.

It *was* robbery, as the Stoat had said just before the Fox came: a stately home in the area whose owner was not in residence at the moment—"Just the thing for us," said the Barn Rat with a cackle—packed full of paintings and fancy vases and ormolu clocks and silverware and fine hangings and *objets de vértu*. There was rumored to be a really excellent cellar, and some exotic orchids in the greenhouse well worth a look-see; and as for the master's bedroom, it was reputed to be something pretty special: "There's supposed to be a canopy 'eld up by griffins, and at the center, up top, a winged Toad, a-carrying a globe," explained the Stoat.

"That's *my* house!" said the Toad indignantly.

Fifteen minutes later, the Toad and the Rabbit were locked up in the barn's tack room, with no way out. The Rabbit had struggled a little but they had only, in the nicest possible way, taken away her pocketknife (but they left her reticule), and escorted her to the tack room. Everyone was very polite, and the Head Weasel who had winked at her looked very sorry about the whole thing, and said, "Never you fear, lass, we'll get you 'ome!" though the Fox, overhearing this, had only laughed in what the Rabbit felt was a very nasty way.

The Toad had not seemed to notice that he was being dragged to a cell: he was too busy shouting, "You—bounders! You—cads, you blackguards! Rob *my* house? The nerve of it!" until they had pushed him through the door and locked it behind him, whereon he had repeatedly hurled himself full length at it, pounding and screaming until he flopped back onto the floor, winded.

"O, why did you say anything?" the Rabbit said. "Toad, I don't mean to be critical, but that was foolish to just pipe up like that!"

He sat up. "Didn't you hear them? They were going to rob my house! The hangings! The silverware! My collection of medals! Burglars!"

"But, Toad, you could have stopped them!" said the Rabbit. "We could have broken into the house with them— they should have taken us right to it!—and then you could have locked them all into the cellar—"

"But my wines!" interjected the Toad with a moan.

"—and then we might have summoned the Badger and everyone, and had them red-handed! Why, you might even have gotten a pardon for capturing them!"

The Toad looked up at her with dawning realization. "You're right! You—are—right! Rabbit, that would have solved everything! O, I *am* a foolish Toad!" And a first tear rolled down his cheek.

"No!" the Rabbit said sternly. "You cannot cry just now, dear Toad. I must listen, and I can't hear anything if you are caterwauling."

"Caterwauling?" gasped the Toad. *"I?"* But she only made a *shh*ing gesture and knelt by the door with one long ear pressed to the tack-room keyhole.

Out in the main room, the Stoats and Weasels, the Barn Rat, and the Fox had returned to their counsels. The house-breaking plan had been a pip, but *this*— the rich Mr Toad, fallen into their hands; it was by way of a honey-fall, everyone agreed— had potential of an entirely different order. China and silver tea sets were all very well in their way, but they had to be carted away and then they had to be fenced, and no one ever gave fair value for stolen goods, and the portioning out was always a nuisance, not to mention there was always the possibility that the police and Scotland Yard might (for a novelty) find them.

In contrast: ransom! Toad of Toad Hall was rich, of course. That meant bags and bags of little gold guineas: easy to divide, easy to carry about with one, easy (once it was broken into smaller coins) to buy rum and tobacco and nice meals at inns with. One could even take one's earnings and emigrate to America, where playing fast and loose with the law did not seem to be so much of a problem as it was here.

"Or," said the Fox, and they all fell silent. Behind the Rabbit, the Toad was still muttering to himself, and the Rabbit made another frantic gesture.

"Or," said the Fox again, and his voice was smooth, "we could turn this Toad and the Rabbit into the authorities."

The Rabbit's gasp was lost in the much louder sensation among the gang members: "What—Scotland Yard!" "That'll be the day, guv'nor!" "Ye'r joking, right?"

The Fox said silkily, "Hear me out. I have been reading the newspapers." The Weasels and Stoats fell silent in respect. Reading! Their own boss, reading! "This Toad did not lie: he is a great felon, and he is on the run from Town, where he is wanted by the police and Scotland Yard. My plan is this: we extract a ransom from the Toad's friends (for I suppose he must have some), and then we turn him over to the authorities anyway, in exchange for a blanket pardon for our own crimes."

There was an awed silence. Eventually one of the Stoats said reverently, "Boss, you're the tops, that's all. I take off my 'at to you"—which he did.

"I dunno," said the Head Weasel doubtfully. "It don't seem right. 'Is friends'll spend all their money to get this 'ere Toad back, and then they don't get 'im after all! It seems dishonest, like. And what about this 'ere Rabbit? She seems all caught in everything accidental-like, and she's a nice young thing."

"Of course we shall free her and let her find her way safely home." The Rabbit, overhearing this, shivered, for there was something not quite reassuring about his tone. The Fox continued, "It will be the *Toad's* money that frees him, not his friends'. If the Toad goes into prison (as he will when we have handed him over), his goods would all be seized and given to the Crown, anyway."

"So *we* might as well 'ave 'em," said one of the Stoats practically. "That makes sense, that does." There was a general assent: gold *and* a pardon; it was practically Christmas morning.

"Good," said the Fox, and stood up. "I'll go now, and write letters to the Toad's friends and to Scotland Yard, putting things in train. We'll be rich, boys, you'll see."

Chapter Nine
Mole and Beryl

Back at the River Bank, things did not change. Nothing was heard of the Toad and the Rabbit. There was a short flurry of articles when the wrecked Dustley was turned into the authorities by a farmer and his mother, but the newspapers gave no sign that they had been captured since, and there were no letters from the Hills reporting their arrival. It was assumed that they were still at large somewhere, doing something, no one knew what, and gradually everyone returned to their lives, from the idlest and most gossipy of Mice to the severe Badger, who returned to his rambling underground grotto in the Wild Wood. It was summer, high summer, and the fields stood tall with ripening grain. The orchard trees sagged under the weight of new fruit, and the gardens were lush with cucumbers and kales and lettuces that seemed to grow under one's eyes. There was work to do, for with high summer came a rising awareness of deep winter to come, and everyone was busy.

"Bother old Toad," the Water Rat said to the Mole one fine afternoon. His lovely boat had been growing a bit dingy, so he had pulled it onto the dock early that morning and examined it, and in the end, even though it was not the season, he decided to scrape and repaint it. Tasks that seem like a good idea first thing on a cool morning always seem much less so in the middle of a hot afternoon, when one feels one has already put in quite a lot of work and yet the task is not done and is not likely to be done for many more hours. It was this that was making him feel testy. He was bent over the hull, laying brushloads of thick paint along its planks. Quite a bit had ended up on his fur as well, so that his glossy greyness was speckled with white. The Mole had offered to help and been turned down on the theory that there was no point their both getting hot and dirty; but he had remained, to run such errands as the Water Rat needed done, to pour out glasses of water or ginger beer as directed by the Rat, and generally to offer entertainment and moral support.

"Toad?" exclaimed the Mole now. "Has he been heard from at last?"

"Not him," snorted the Water Rat. "The newspapers all say he could be anywhere and so he could, and that dratted Rabbit with him. Anyway, I am off. As soon as I am done with this"—he gestured with his paintbrush, splashing white onto the dock and into the River, a thick thread that dissolved into a white smear spreading downstream—"I must be off to visit my cousins."

"Ratty, you can't, not with everything so unsettled!" cried the Mole. "Toad gone—Badger gone—Otter still at the seaside!"

"I can," said the Water Rat. "I have already delayed far too long—an unavoidable visit to some cousins down south. But, Moley, there's nothing we *can* do here, anyway. And *you'll* still be around to hold down the fort. Keep the Stoats out of Toad Hall and so forth."

"I suppose," said the Mole, but his tone was despondent. "Ratty, you will be quick, won't you?"

"As quick as I can," the Water Rat said. "But—family. If it comes to it, you can always ask old Badger for help. He won't like being taken away from the Wild Wood, not at this time of year and with the Weasels getting uppity again, but he'll understand."

The Water Rat left early the next day, and the Mole suddenly found himself as close to alone and idle as anyone could be, who lived on the River Bank in summertime. He had meant to do some paddling about on his own, practicing his skills away from the Water Rat's kindly amusement, and perhaps learning a little more of the River's secret life, but he couldn't stop worrying about where the Toad might be—and, he had to admit, the Rabbit. She and Beryl might be ruining the tenor of life on the River Bank, but that didn't mean he thought she should be imprisoned for something that was undoubtedly entirely the Toad's fault.

Mindful of his promise to the Water Rat, that afternoon he rowed up to Toad Hall in the new-painted boat (and very white it was now; it cast brilliant flashing reflections that caught his eye as he worked), and tied it off in the boathouse with some satisfaction; he had sculled the whole way without once splashing water into the boat.

He walked up the bright lawn to the quiet house. No one answered when he rang the front bell, nor when he went back to the servants' entrance by the kitchen and knocked there. Such household staff as the Toad kept seemed to be entirely gone, though the Mole didn't know where or why, whether they were stealing holidays or seeking new positions, or had been sent away until such time as the Toad returned (if he ever did). Well, the Badger had keys to Toad Hall, so if things went on too long, the Mole could always go into the Wild Wood (but in daylight, and not straying from the path) and retrieve them. For now, he just walked around the exterior, peeking in the tall windows to see whether there were any signs of Stoats or other vagabonds inside. But the rooms were orderly, safe, untouched, still. With the sunlight slanting in, everything looked as though it were dozing, conserving its energy for its master's return.

He was still anxious, so he walked across the fields to his own little home, a couple of miles away. He had been staying with the Water Rat all this summer, and only been back to Mole End for short stops, to pick up a formal waistcoat for Toad's tea party with Beryl and the Rabbit, and to retrieve a fishing pole. There hadn't been enough time to do more than glance about. Probably there was nothing wrong, he reassured himself, but it wouldn't hurt just to check.

His thoughts turned this way and that as he marched across the fields and through the hedgerows, always coming back to the Toad and the Rabbit. Had they been secretly captured and imprisoned? Where *were* they? Had they made it to the Hills? If not, what *had* happened to them? Why had they not at least sent news? But he had no answers, no answers at all.

Mole End was a underground residence, tucked into a copse in the middle of a field planted with oats: small but perfectly sized for a gregarious animal who liked guests but loved living alone. It was cool in the summer and easy to warm in the winter; a bit shabby but his own, and filled with familiar things: worn furniture, a shelf with a few beloved books; his slippers, placed neatly before the little cupboard bed, which was covered with the quilt his mother had made for him. On the wall over the fireplace was a sampler sewn by one of his sisters when he had first moved to the River Bank, so long ago: trees bracketing a row of Moles in silhouette. They were meant to depict his family, but she had added several extra Moles, to fill out the line. Beneath them were the words AUDACIA BONA, MELIOR DOMUS DULCIS.

There was nothing troubling to note, no mouse holes in the pantry walls or places where the ceiling was developing a leak. A thin layer of dust had settled upon everything, and he picked up his feather duster to brush it away. But there *was* something. He stood in the center of the room for a moment with the duster drooping from one paw. What was it? And then it came to him. Just as Toad Hall had been asleep, Mole End was asleep, empty of his living presence, and it had taken the opportunity to close in upon itself, to grow still for a time, to slumber. Things rested where they had been put away, and even the kitchen knife laid upon the counter and the old pack of cards sitting in the center of the little table felt unchangeable, untouched and untouchable. He felt an invader, a spy in his own home.

He could wake his home up, he knew. Mole End would welcome him as it always did, gladly, generously forgiving him for being gone so long. But to what purpose? He would only leave it again, and for a time it would long for his presence, like a dog left behind on market day, cocking an ear to the door and pacing restlessly until it finally gave up again and returned to slumber, to kill the time until its master's return.

There would come a day in a few weeks, when summer began to release her hold on the hot dusty fields and the glittering River, when he *would* return, and open the windows and turn out the bed, cut bread for sandwiches, build playing-card houses, read books, wear slippers, and sleep long, night after night: but that was not yet. So he put down the feather duster (and it too went back to sleep as he did so, and became part of the dreaming house), and slipped up the graveled tunnel, and out.

Wrapped in his thoughts, the Mole returned to Toad's boathouse and then rowed back to the Rat's hole. He chanced to look up from his brown study as he passed Sunflower Cottage. The first lights were on inside.

"How I wish Ratty were here!" he said to himself as he secured the boat. "He's just the chap for this sort of brooding—musings about home—poetry and suchlike. And for having some tea brewed up and maybe a sandwich or two for a chap when he gets home from a long day," he added sadly, for of course there was no such thing awaiting him.

Mole sighed. He unlatched the little door to let himself in, started the fire and put a kettle on and put out the tea things. As he waited for the water to boil, he picked up the Water Rat's post from the little basket below the brass-edged slot in the door and flipped through it, for he was having his own letters forwarded here. But there was nothing for him: only a letter for the Water Rat, some circulars, and a catalog of canaries and songbirds that might be purchased through the mails—and then he saw it: a single mysterious envelope.

He turned it over in his paws. It was of cheap, thin, yellowish paper, none too clean, but it was addressed intriguingly:

To any Friend of TOAD OF TOAD HALL,
The River Bank
The River, &c.,

URGENT—to be opened
IMMEDIATELY on receipt

—A MATTER OF LIFE & DEATH!!!

Beside this, the postmaster had written in his tiny, fussy script: *To the Water Rat's—Everyone else is away.* The postmark, alas, was blurred.

The Mole opened it and read the contents. "It's no use," he said unhappily. "I shall have to go speak with Beryl."

The Mole took the kettle off and banked the fire—for he knew that one should *never* leave a fire unattended, and so ought you—and walked quickly to Sunflower Cottage with the envelope clutched tight in one paw. It was full dark when he got there. The windows had been closed against the mist that was rising from the River. The curtains pulled over them glowed warmly from within, but beside the door a gaslight shaped like an old mail-coach lamp shone brightly. He took a deep breath, put his paw on the bell-pull, and tugged.

Something chimed inside. He wondered whether there was time to run away unobserved, but the door opened almost immediately, letting out warm golden light, and there was Beryl. "Why—Mole!" she exclaimed, and her eyes were bright with surprise and curiosity. "What are you doing here? Come in!"

The Rubicon had been crossed. The Mole followed her through the door and into the parlor, which was papered in lilac and white stripes, with many framed photographs clustered across every flat surface, and filled with comfortable-looking furniture upholstered in a rich, buttery yellow. There was a fire in the grate, and a green-shaded lamp hung over Beryl's writing desk. He could see her fountain pen laid across a half-written page; clearly she had been working.

"Thank you," said the Mole awkwardly. "What a, ah, pleasant room. Very . . . homey."

"Thank you," she said and smiled something that was very like a grin. Was she laughing at him? Morosely, he rather feared so. "Would you like tea, Mole? Have you eaten anything? I saw you out on the River earlier, and I know the Water Rat is gone. I was just going to the kitchen to make a little something."

The Mole realized he *was* in fact famished. "Thank you," he said meekly. He trailed Beryl into the kitchen, and found it as cheery as the parlor had been: copper pots and bright earthenware on shelves, and onions and hams hanging from the rafters.

She put a kettle on and said conversationally, "The Mole at Sunflower Cottage! Wonders never cease. You've been avoiding me ever since I came to the River Bank, haven't you?"

The Mole shuffled his paws a little. "I know, and I'm sorry, but—well—I thought you were just here to . . . be a nuisance. . . . *You* know. Watch over me and . . . report back home . . . and so forth."

Beryl sounded a little hurt when she replied, "You thought I was here to *spy?* As though I had nothing better to do with my life!" She was slicing bread for bread-and-butter, but she managed to toss her head.

For Beryl and the Mole were sister and brother. Beryl was the eldest, and when they had been children, back in the Hills together, she had bossed him around rather. To be fair, everyone had: he was the youngest, with five older siblings, not to mention his parents (before they had died) and any number of concerned aunts and severe uncles—everyone with her or his own notion of what the Mole needed to be doing with himself. When the time had come to leave home, he had scrimped and saved, and at last collected enough money to buy Mole End, which was humble but entirely his own, and pleasantly distant from all of them. "Why *are* you here, then?" he said in a small voice.

Beryl began bustling about, finding tea and pots and cups and sugar and milk and shortcake and crumpets and butter and marmalade. "I love them all dearly, but everyone was always wanting me to decide things and plan things and fix things, and telling me exactly how I ought to be. I just wanted to live in a little house—my *own* little house: no nieces or nephews come for extended visits!—and write; so as soon as I was able to save enough, away I went. And dear Rabbit was longing for an adventure of her own, so I invited her to come with me."

"I see. But why not elsewhere?" the Mole pursued, still a little suspicious. "Why the River Bank? You knew I lived here."

She poured loose tea into a pot. "You made it sound so lovely in your letters—green, and busy, and beautiful, and— and the River! We had nothing like that at home, did we? I wanted to see it, that's all." She looked up, meeting his eyes. "And I—thought it might be nice to be close to someone I knew, but I knew you wouldn't eternally be fussing at me. You were always my favorite brother."

"I *was*?" The Mole gaped at her. "When you were always dragging me off places and scolding me not to get in trouble?"

"Of course, silly! Why do you think I was always taking you along everywhere I went? I was—" she began; but at that moment, the kettle began to whistle. "Tea! Do you still take milk, Mole, dear?"

It was all very like a dream, but a dream that included tea and quite a splendid supper. Back in the parlor a few minutes later, Beryl said, a bit stickily (she had been eating crumpets toasted in the fire and drizzled with honey), "I didn't even ask, I was so happy to see you—*why* did you finally come to call?"

"O, Beryl!" In the happiness of catching up with his sister, the Mole had for a few minutes forgotten his distress. He put down his cup on the little table at which they were seated. "It's Toad! I am a terrible fellow, Beryl—I forgot for a moment, but it's the horridest thing. Toad has been kidnapped! Here is the letter."

She took it from him, and together they read it:

> To Any TRUE Friend of Mr Toad—
> The notoreous Mr Toad after his recent criminal activities has fallen into our hands and we are holding him to ransom. One of you must leave 50,000 ~~sour~~ _pounds in gold_ under THE ELM TREE behind St Giles—or else! Come _ALONE!_ Do not tell Scotland Yard!! Or ELSE!!
>
> P.S. We also have his young friend the Rabbit whom we will free for only £100 as she is a very nice young lady and not rich like him.
>
> P.S.S. _COME ALONE OR ELSE_

At the bottom was drawn a little tombstone.

Beryl eyed the ransom note critically. "This is not a very good ransom note at all! It does not tell us _when_ we are to leave the money, nor _which_ St Giles—they must mean a church or chapel, I would think, for all they are so imprecise! Nor does it tell us what will happen if we do not comply. The tombstone is a nice detail, but—"

The Mole said sternly, "Beryl! Now is no time to get all—all _authoressy!_ They have the Toad and the Rabbit!"

Her forehead crinkled, ruffling the smooth dark fur. "I know, I know, only—I should have written a much better one, if I were them. Everything spelled properly, for one thing."

But the kind-hearted Mole exclaimed in an agony, "Who *cares* how well they spell? What are we to do? *That's* the thing! The Water Rat is gone, and the Badger is away as well—*and* the Otter—and there is no one at Toad Hall to speak with, or to tell us who in Town could aid us—" He had worked himself into a fine frenzy, speaking faster and faster, and he jumped to his feet, wringing his paws. "What can we *do?* Beryl, there must be something!"

She was running one paw around the rim of her teacup, frowning at it unseeing. "I do see what you are saying, and I apologize, dear Mole. It's always so easy to get, well, distracted. We do not know when they expect the money— which we cannot in any case get; really, these villains are not very sensible! They ought to have tortured Toad until they got his bankers' name in Town—I know, I know," she said hastily as he opened his mouth again. "But we do know *where* they will expect it: St Giles's churchyard."

"But *which* St Giles?" said the Mole mournfully. "I am sure there are churches called St Giles all over the country. Why, there was one in our own old neighborhood, near the Hills."

Beryl exclaimed, "Exactly! Toad and dear Rabbit *were* on their way to the Hills, and that's where they were captured! I am sure of it! So all we have to do is go out there and find them, and perhaps we may free them."

The Mole and Beryl made plans to leave at first light—"For there's no good we can do, travelling at night," said Beryl, and the Mole, hearing an Owl in the distance, had shivered and agreed. He was up late into the night, packing: unearthing the Water Rat's pistols from the bottom of a trunk and then checking one over; selecting a cutlass from the display of crossed weapons upon the wall above the mantel and sharpening it; finding bandages (which might be needed), and a blanket roll and a tent (Beryl was bringing the provisions and her own blankets); and then realizing it would not all fit his knapsack and needed to be winnowed. At last he had everything selected and his pack strapped closed. He stood up, puffing and sweaty, and realized his spare clean handkerchiefs were on the table where he had put them during the packing, so he had to open everything and find a corner somewhere for *them*; and then he couldn't remember whether he had accidentally packed the compass or merely mislaid it; and *then*—anyway, it was very late when he at last was able to make himself ready for bed.

He was in bed and about to blow out his candle when he remembered one more thing. "O, *bother*," said the Mole aloud, dismally. "I must write a letter to Badger and Ratty—*two* letters, blast it!—telling them what's what, so they can work out the ransom and follow us as soon as they may." Forcing his eyes open, he dragged himself from bed and wrote the letters. Putting the Badger's note into an envelope, he placed a stamp upon it and tucked it into the mail slot for the next day; but the Water Rat's letter he folded over and writing *RATTY— VERY IMPORTANT!* across the back in large, firm letters, he placed it in the middle of the table where it was sure to be seen; and then, finally, *finally,* he went off to sleep.

There was just one thing he overlooked, in his fatigue and worry for his friend: he forgot to include the original ransom note in his letter to the Rat. He had it upon the desk as he wrote; but as he reread what he had written, he absently folded it and slid it back into his coat pocket, where it remained through the rest of these adventures, unfound and unremembered.

Just before dawn the next morning, Beryl and the Mole met at the foot of her lawn, beneath the chestnut tree. They each bore a knapsack and carried a sturdy walking stick, and Beryl had a Survey map tucked into her pocket. They consulted in soft voices for a moment, and then Beryl patted the Mole's hand, and they walked together northward along the river path.

They were observed by a Moorhen, a Mouse, and a Hedgehog: gossips, all.

The Water Rat returned to the River Bank late that same night. In an ordinary year (for this was an annual visit), he might have walked home, ambling along back lanes and across cow fields, pausing to try the local brews whenever he came to a particularly promising tavern, and sleeping nights beneath the stars, perhaps even seeing a meteor shower (for this was August); but the Toad was missing (and the Rabbit), so he stayed for as short a period as could in courtesy be managed, and then returned upon the train—though in general, the animals of the River Bank (except for Toad) avoided such things.

He was let off at their little country station in the village very late, the only one to disembark onto the abandoned platform. There were no porters, and even the stationmaster did not make an appearance. He could hear crickets and frogs in the darkness, and bright halos of insects and moths fluttered about the station's tin-shaded lamps. Otherwise everything was still.

"Rat!" said a voice from the shadows.

"Ho," said the Water Rat cautiously.

The Badger stepped into the cone of light cast by one of the station lanterns. The Water Rat relaxed. "Badger, you should know better than to sneak up on a fellow late at night!"

The Badger only shook his ponderous head, looking severe. "I have been meeting each train, hoping you would be arriving this way."

"Badger, there was no need for that! Or— O Badger, do you mean you've heard something?" he asked urgently. "About Toad, I mean?"

"No, nothing," said the Badger. "But outdoors and at night is no time for discussions. We'll go to your house and talk there."

The Water Rat peppered the Badger with questions during the walk home. About the Toad, there was nothing to tell: he had *not* been apprehended, so far as was known. Nor was the Rabbit anywhere to be found. "And after so many days with no news . . ." The Badger trailed off. There was no need to complete the sentence, and in any case, it was not their way to speculate about such things.

The Water Rat unlocked his front door and let them into his little parlor, which was dark and cold, the wicks on the lanterns burnt down to nothing. "Mole?" called the Rat. "Mole?"

"Then it is true," said the Badger heavily.

The Water Rat lit a candle so that he could see, and pulled down one of the lanterns to trim its wick. "*What's* true? Has he gone back to Mole End?"

The Badger cleared his throat as though preparing to relate dark news: "It's as I feared. No, Rat: Mole has *not* returned to Mole End. They have eloped."

The Water Rat gaped at him. "Eloped? *Who* has eloped?"

"Mole and the young Mole lady. Beryl. I had hoped there was another interpretation of the facts, but there is not.

Mole's absence proves it. They are gone, Beryl and the Mole together."

"I simply don't believe it," said the Water Rat, finding his voice at last.

"No? Read this." The Badger shoved a piece of paper into the Rat's paw.

Dear Badger,
I am writing in great haste to tell you that Beryl and I are off together to St Giles's (which is the church closest to the Hills), as soon as we can go. Perhaps together we can fix the worst plight ever two animals found themselves in. I'm very sorry, but we're leaving you to sort out the money as we know nothing of lawyers or bank-managers. I've left the original letter at Ratty's so you can see what has to happen.

I hope this finds you in good health. I checked on Toad Hall today and all seemed well enough there.

Yours &c.,
the Mole

P.S. Beryl sends her regards.

The Water Rat flipped the note over, looking for something, anything, upon the back, but it was blank. "That cannot be right! This makes no sense at all. Where's this letter to me that he writes about?"

They found the Mole's letter to the Rat upon the table and read it together. It said essentially the same thing: the Mole and Beryl were fled together to a church in the Hills; they would be back in a few day's time; someone needed to do something or other about the money. There was no enclosed letter.

"'The money' must be a dowry, I suppose," said the Badger. He tapped the sheet of paper with one paw. "And this letter the Mole refers to—it must be a note from Beryl to him."

"Perhaps she has run into financial difficulties and must marry to repair her fortune?" hazarded the Water Rat.

"Mole is not rich," the Badger reminded him.

"I know, only— Mole . . . in . . . love! I should hardly have thought it. If they have exchanged more than a word or two, I never saw it."

"We have all been very busy with this Toad business. Have you been with Mole every moment?"

"No, of course not! I am not his nursemaid, and he has his own activities, just as we all do." The Water Rat frowned. "Beryl! Why, he does not even like her!"

"That is the way these things work," the Badger said grimly. "Have you never read a serialized story in the newspaper?"

"No, and I have a hard time believing that you have!" replied the Water Rat in surprise.

The Badger continued, unheeding. "They are full—full!— of young people who dislike one another upon first meeting, and then through a sequence of misadventures fall in love. These stories invariably"—he repeated it for the full effect— "*invariably,* end with a wedding."

The Water Rat gasped. "A wedding! O Badger, surely it will not come to that! Marriage!"

"I should have said such doings were not his kind of thing at all, no, "said the Badger grimly. "I mean no offense against Beryl, who is a very pleasant animal—in fact, admirable in many ways—but—*you* know."

The Water Rat did know. "Badger, we cannot allow him to make a mistake like this! Can he not be stopped?"

"How?" mourned the Badger. "It is most inconsiderate of them to leave without warning like this, just now, when things are in such disorder on the River Bank. We cannot afford to leave, yet we shall have to follow them and try to talk sense into them."

The Water Rat said in a bleak tone, "I suppose we must. I say, Badger, what about Toad? He is still out there somewhere, or might be, anyway."

"*Bother* Toad!" said the Badger savagely. "I wash my hands of him. How many times have we warned him his foolish misdeeds would disgrace him utterly (if not worse); and this time, to cap it off, he has sucked Another—an innocent!— into his orbit." He looked up with dawning horror. "I *say*. They must be married, as well!"

The Water Rat gaped back. "Toad? And the *Rabbit?*"

The Badger groaned. "It hardly bears thinking of, but they have been days and *days* together."

"If they return to the River Bank, he must of course marry her," said the Rat. "But it might steady him, you know."

But the Badger shook his head and said only, in a low voice, "Toad, wed. It almost makes one hope he *doesn't* return."

Chapter Ten
"Cribbed, Cabined, and Confined"

The Toad was useless. All the valiant courage to which he rather liked to lay claim had evaporated, and through that first long night, as the gang of outlaws made their plans and the Fox wrote his letters, the Toad could only huddle against a wall in the old barn's tack room, fat tears rolling down his face and moaning "Doomed! Doomed!" at regular intervals, like a fog-horn. After a few vain attempts to soothe him, the Rabbit settled down to listening for whatever she might hear through the cracked and slatted walls, though it was little enough: low talk and rude laughter.

The pale light before dawn was beginning to ease in through the cracks in the walls when the Fox at last said, more loudly, "So that's the plan, boys. Everyone clear?" There were sounds of assent. "*You* will take the letters to the post. *You* and *you* will stand guard, and we'll gather again tomorrow night. We can't hear anything for a day or two, so for now, it's just— keep them safe and secure, right, boys?"

"Right, guv'nor, right," said several voices. After a general shuffling and "See you later, chaps"-ing, the barn door opened and closed, and then the Rabbit heard the door to their prison unlocked.

It was the Fox. "Nice and comfy?" he said in his smooth voice.

Surprisingly, it was the Toad who responded. He looked a wretched thing, tear-stained and filthy, his natty Town-going clothes torn and disreputable and scattered with straw from the barn floor; but he had managed to stand up, and, leaning heavily upon a stool, he said in a thin voice, "Do you mean to starve us? Villain, do your worst!"

The Fox shook his head. "Starve—? O no—where *are* my manners?" He gestured and the assigned guards stepped forward—the Rabbit was relieved to note that one was the amiable Head Weasel who had winked at her, but the other was one of the larger Stoats, who had been rude earlier. "Boys, we don't want our guests to starve, do we?"

The Stoat laughed, not at all nicely.

The Fox continued, "Find some water and food for them, and then keep them locked up tight until we return. I should be very sorry if anything, *anything at all*"—and here he glared at the Stoat, who looked surly and kicked his paw at the ground—"were to happen to them before I returned. Don't get stupid, and if we do this right we'll be rich—rich and pardoned!" And with a sweeping (but not, the Rabbit thought, very sincere) bow, he melted into the cool shadows of approaching dawn, and the door was swung shut on them. A few minutes later the Weasel brought them some coarse brown bread and a bit of butter, and a pail of water that was not very clean, with bits of straw floating on the surface. "Sorry it's not what you're used to, lass," he said apologetically to the Rabbit, "but tonight I'll run over to the tuck-shop in the village and bring you back sponge cakes and jelly, and won't *that* be a treat?" Then the door was locked, and they were left alone again.

"Well, that's that, then," said the Rabbit practically, and turned to the Toad. "We must escape, that's all, and *then* we shall go to the Hills."

But the Toad was turning over the coarse bread as though hoping to find a slice of roast beef hiding beneath it. He looked up and said mournfully, "They *do* mean to starve us to death, after all. But what can we do?"

That was the question. The next two days were dreary beyond the pen's ability to tell—not with enthusiasm, at any rate. With the Toad's listless aid, the Rabbit went over their cell inch by inch. The tack room's walls were of sturdy oak, over a century old, their wood aged into rock-like solidity; and, while there were gaps, they were none of them narrow enough for a Rabbit in walking-dress, let alone a stoutish Toad reluctant to lose his buttons. The floor was crowded with saddle racks, tack trunks, wooden stools (one with a broken leg), and pails. Against one side wall was a large wooden box lined with tin ("A coffin," moaned the Toad) that was used to store sacks of oats for mash. There was a stack of horse blankets in another corner ("What a lucky chance!" said the Rabbit; "Shrouds," groaned the Toad: *dusty* shrouds!"). Just out of reach, there was a cluttered single shelf, and beyond that, the tack room stretched far, far up to a slatted ceiling that was the floor of the haymow. The walls were hung with saddles, riding whips ("Implements of torture," wept the Toad), bridles, cinches, straps of leather, spare steel bits, and soft hempen halters; but everything was quite out of their grasp, even were they to jump. In any case neither was of the athletic, vigorous build that makes nothing of leaping gorges or scaling sheer rock faces.

"Doomed," said the Toad sadly, and threw himself to the ground weeping. "Doomed!"

"Nonsense!" said the Rabbit stoutly. "Why should we be doomed? The worst thing that may happen is that they will receive their ransom and free us; and that will be that."

But the Toad could only roll about and say, "It's not fair; it's not fair!"

The Rabbit knelt beside him. "*What's* not fair? Being kidnapped? I am sure you are right, but here we are and we must make the best of it."

But just at that moment it was not the kidnapping that so inflamed his sensibilities. It was the ransom. "Did you hear them?" sobbed the Toad. "Fifty—thousand—pounds! I shall be bankrupt!" (This was not at all true.) "I shall be begging in the street—eating shoe leather—sleeping in parks in all weather—" (This was even less true.) "It can't be done, Rabbit, that's all."

But the Rabbit said reasonably, "Well, it is your own money; what better use for it than to ransom yourself?"

"It's the *principle*," wept the Toad. "They should have asked someone else for the money! My admiring friends! These brigands could have insisted a collection be taken up. I am sure everyone would have helped out a bit. Instead, they want my last groat!" He threw out a grand gesture. "Perhaps they want the *teeth* from my *head*?"

"Keep it down in there," one of the guards called through the door in a warning tone. "We can't 'ear ourselves count our points, we can't"—for they were playing cribbage on an overturned pail to while away what looked to be a long, weary day.

"Toad—*Toad!*" said the Rabbit, sounding a little strained: even she had her limits. "Toad, you *can't* expect your friends to pay for your ransom when you have so much money! It's—it's absurd."

The Toad was still sniffling. "I should have thought they would be happy to help in every little way—selling a field or two—cashing in their Funds—borrowing from lenders in out-of-the-way little offices in Town—but—" He stopped suddenly, an arrested expression on his face. "No. In fact, I am come by my just desserts. Badger told me he would wash his hands of me—Ratty, too! Even Moley looked disapproving, the last time I got in trouble, and said—he said—"The Toad choked. "He said they couldn't keep bailing me out of my troubles. The best of friends—the truest chaps a fellow ever knew! I have worn out their affection, that's all!"

"Toad," the Rabbit said with a sigh, her paws pressed against her closed eyes, for she seemed to be developing a headache. "Your friends shall get the ransom note, and they shall speak with your banker, who shall collect the funds and pay the ransom, and You. Shall. Be. Freed."

"Unless they get the ransom note, and decide *not* to," said the Toad in a dejected tone, determined to be wretched. "They may be grateful to have me gone. Life will be simpler on the River Bank without me. It's just what I deserve."

"*If* that happens—which it will *not*—we'll just have to escape," said the Rabbit practically.

"Impossible," sobbed the Toad. "Detained—penned— caged, like a wild beast! Doomed! No way out—no hope— no—"

"What?" said the Rabbit. "You're *Toad*! What prison has *ever* held you?"

The Toad shook his head violently and shrieked, "Doomed!"

Rabbit knelt beside him. "Dear Toad, they write you up in newspapers! Bold Toad, adventuresome Toad! Acts of Parliament are written because of you! There have been widespread prison reforms because of you!"

The Toad raised his head and said, still a little reluctant to relinquish his misery, "I suppose you are right."

"Why, you are practically a legend!" said the Rabbit. "Of course there shall be a way for us to escape."

"How did you escape last time?" asked the Rabbit. It was the next day. By degrees, the Rabbit had restored the Toad's *amour propre*, but (as was usually the case with the Toad) he did not long remain there, instead sliding immediately past equipoise and into the divine egoism one most commonly associated with him.

The Toad said complacently, "The prison warden's daughter admired me rather—my person or my character or my courage, *I* can't say—a pretty young thing—smitten, quite smitten—but the difference between our stations was too great; in any case, I could not reciprocate her understandable feelings. . . ." He trailed off with a self-satisfied smile that was not at all attractive. "Where was I?"

"The warden's daughter," prompted the Rabbit.

"Yes, yes," said the Toad, with a little bow, as though he were speaking to a political assembly. "To be brief, then. It was for love, though I blush to say it—" (he did no such thing) "—that this warden's daughter coaxed an agèd washerwoman to give me her clothes. I disguised myself—walked down corridors lined with guards—through gates overseen by cruel turnkeys—chaffed policemen to their faces—mocked the warden directly—no one guessed a thing! He, he! I walked right through the front gates, bold as brass and free as a bird!"

He meant to go on a bit more, but the Rabbit was not attending. She said, "I don't *think* the Weasel or the Stoat have any daughters that might fall in love with you, and I doubt there are any washerwomen at all associated with this barn." She looked disapprovingly at the filthy horse blankets.

"I suppose you're right," said the Toad, a little quenched. "But, wait— Rabbit, has not the Weasel been making up to *you?*"

"Me? Surely not!" exclaimed the Rabbit. "He's quite old! I mean, he has been quite kind, true, but I am sure that's all he means by it! And if it *is* true"—and she *did* have the grace to blush—"it does seem hard to take advantage of his sentiments like this, as it would leave him in the most *terrible* trouble with the Fox and his fellows. Still, I suppose we must make the attempt, mustn't we?"

Now that it was broad daylight, it was possible to see a little of the barn's main floor through a chink in the wall, though it was nearly the dullest sight imaginable. For a long while, the Weasel and the Stoat played cards, until the Weasel won ("And that is good," said the Rabbit, "for it shall make his mood better."); and then the Weasel went out to stretch his legs and have a smoke while the Stoat remained, tossing his knife point-first into the floor; and then they sat together for a time saying not much; but finally the Stoat said, "Well, I'll go out for a bit of a walk. Don't you fall asleep while I'm gone, 'ear? I don't want to come back and find these desprit crim'nals 'ave 'it you on the 'ead and run off," and he laughed and left.

"Now!" hissed the Toad.

"I *know*," responded the Rabbit in a whisper. "It's just— O, all right, if I *must*." As the Toad laid himself on a pallet of horse blankets and began to snore discreetly, she tapped softly on the tack-room door.

"Hello?" she said.

She heard the Weasel approach. He said through the door, "Why, lass! Awake? Y'oughter be curled up after your long night, a-sleeping the day away, a-dreaming of pretty 'ats and cakes, an' nice things like that."

"Cake," moaned the Toad behind her. But very softly.

The Rabbit said, "O, I would, but— I am so *very* afraid! What will happen to us when this is done? I know the Fox says we shall be freed, but how can we trust that? I am sure something quite terrible will happen!"

"Nothing'll 'appen to you!" the Weasel said in a comforting tone. "This 'ere Toad's friends'll show up with the money, and that'll be that—you'll be free!"

The Rabbit gave a little sob. It did not sound at all convincing to her, but the Weasel said miserably, "O, lassie! No, you'll be safe, I swear it to you!"

"It's just that—well, he's a Fox, and—and . . ." She trailed off and sniffed again. *That* sounded better; the Toad nodded enthusiastically and lifted his thumbs to her. She ventured a break in her voice. "Please, sir—please! Is there *nothing* you can do?"

"Well, it's like this," he said slowly, and his voice sounded troubled. "Our Boss is—well, as you noticed, clever girl that you are—a Fox. And Foxes . . . Well, you're right, Foxes isn't like other folks, and 'e wouldn't take kindly to anything 'appening to you, and that's a fact."

"Could you not turn your back for a few moments, even?" she said, striving for a hopeless tone. "I *know* it's too much to ask for; I'm just—" She broke off on another sob. The Toad tried to slap her silently upon the back, but she pushed him away.

"What's this?" said the Stoat, quite loud: he had re-entered the barn unbeknownst to them. "'Aving a chat with the prisoners? Maybe they want feather pillows for their 'eads? Maybe they want *barth* water? A grand idea, I *don't* think."

And that, as they say, was the end of that.

"Now what?" said the Rabbit.

It was the middle of the afternoon. The barn was cool and shady, but when the prisoners pressed their eyes to the chinks in the outside wall, they could see the sun blazing brilliantly outside, spangling on the pollen that hung everywhere in the air. There had been a low-voiced altercation between the Head Weasel and the Stoat, but neither the Toad nor the Rabbit could hear any of it. After that, the Head Weasel did not approach the tack room. The Stoat did not leave the barn again, but stretched himself out against the main door with his cap over his eyes, and they might have thought he was asleep, except that when a fly landed upon his vest, he flicked it away with one leisurely paw.

For an hour, the Toad had lain beside the door, thrashing about and groaning, and the Rabbit had cried out, "O, he is sick! Please, bring a doctor—water—anything!" It was a pity, thought the Rabbit, that they had not tried this first, for their captors did not seem at all convinced, the Stoat only laughing while the Head Weasel, who had evidently resolved his doubts regarding the Rabbit's future well-being to his satisfaction, said from his place across the barn, "Give over, lassie, do! It won't serve you as you'd like, and you'll just make your throat dry to no end."

For a second hour, the Toad had taken a position beside the door and cut wheedle after wheedle. He tried bribes and he tried threats; he tried appeals to reason and to sentiment and to principle; he tried whining and blustering and begging and commanding; but none of it had the effect he had hoped for, the Head Weasel saying little and the Stoat saying only, whenever the Toad paused for breath or effect, "Go on, go on! It's as good a play, it is," and, "I think you're up to Act Three, Scene Two, chum," and, "When's the young lady get a line?"

After that, everyone fell silent, and there the situation rested for a while. The sun crept across the sky, but clouds began to heap beneath it. The light in the barn began to change value, to something cooler, dimmer. And then tap. Tap. Tap, tap. Tap-tap-tap-tap—and it was raining, a steady soft grey noise that laid a hush over everything. The wooden walls seemed to exhale cool air, as though it were seeping through from the outside.

The rain continued, steady, soft, grey, pattering on the slate roof like squirrels' feet. The Stoat and the Head Weasel went back to playing cribbage. The Toad sat forlorn in the middle of the floor, sighing heavily at intervals. The Rabbit examined their prison closely one more time: wooden walls, tack trunks, stools, saddle stands, pails, blankets. She climbed onto the feed box and was able to better examine the single shelf's contents, all the bits and bobs every tack room seems to accumulate: neatsfoot oil and saddle soap, broken stirrup irons, old horseshoes, empty liniment bottles that still smelled sharply of creosote, hoof-picks, a chipped mug lined with a mysterious black residue, a kerosene lantern without a wick, ancient racing calendars, a small yellow paper-covered book entitled *Did She Ever!*, a U-shaped blade for cutting straps and reins and such. None of it would be very useful, but she brought down the strap-cutting blade and the horseshoes. She climbed onto one of the saddle stands to see if she could reach the gear hung from the walls, but there didn't seem to be a way to pull any of it down, certainly not without making a horrible lot of noise.

She returned to the back wall of the tack room. The barn was an old one, and the siding boards had shrunk over the decades so that there were cracks between them, an inch or two wide in places. Air breathed through the chinks, and when she pressed her eye to one of them, she saw a robin, hopping in the little grassy yard behind the barn, pulling for worms, and the beechwood just behind, the pale trunks and shivering leaves lost with distance in the silvering rain. For a moment, she saw a shape deep in the trees, indistinct but tall, slim-legged as it paced deliberately forward, rain sparking off the crown made by its antlers. "O!" murmured the Rabbit.

"What?" said the Toad's voice behind her, sounding surly.

"A stag!" she said. "O, it is the most beautiful thing." She wished Beryl were there with her; Beryl was the one for fancy words.

"Stags! What good are *stags?*" wept the Toad, and flung himself backward. He had been having a trying few days, and his interest in Nature's glories, never great (Nature, in his considered opinion, was rather undersupplied with umbrella'd café tables and sycophantic waiters to bring one a little something to take the heat off), had sagged to a level so slight as to be nonexistent.

The Rabbit sighed to herself and ran her fingers along the wall. At the wall's base, the planks' ends were blunt, eaten away by moisture. but there was not enough of a gap for even a slender Rabbit to slip through, let alone a portly Toad, who would in any case very likely have to be goaded. The feed box had been built against a side wall, leaving a narrow space beside the back wall, and this had gradually been stacked with detritus, but she could see more of the silver daylight behind the pile of oddments. Was there a gap? As silently as she could, the Rabbit heaved aside a broken-backed saddle that smelled of mildew, then a shredded horse blanket. Beneath that were the broken pieces of a manger, much too heavy for her. "Toad?" she said softly. "Would you be so kind as to assist me?"

"Why?" said the Toad: quite rudely, I am sorry to say, and at his normal volume.

She hissed, "Shh! Don't let them hear! The light— I think there's a hole down here! Help me move some of this away."

"Why bother?" said the Toad, again at a normal volume, and then catching on at last: "Ah!" much more softly.

"Pipe down, you," called the Stoat warningly from the main floor of the barn.

Together they managed to remove the manger's pieces, one by one, and the forgiving rain concealed many of the small noises they made, the soft panting, the *sotto voce* crabbing (this was the Toad), and the whispered instructions. Only once was all nearly lost, when the Toad suddenly howled and dropped his end of a plank, which hit the floor with a tremendous clatter. "A ih-eh," he explained around his paw as he sucked upon it, which the Rabbit took to mean *a sliver,* for she had been getting them as well, and they really were *most* uncomfortable.

Scraping of chairs on the main floor; quick footsteps; the door unlocked—the Rabbit, with great presence of mind, had just time enough to toss a ruined horse blanket into the corner to conceal the silver daylight before the Stoat and Head Weasel were standing in the open doorway.

Glancing around, the Stoat gave a mean-spirited laugh and said, "Redecorating, are we?" He entered the room, poking about. "What do you think, Weasel? 'Is 'Ighness might like a divan with crocerdile legs? Ooh, 'ow about a con-*serv*-atory? Or a piano-forte, an' we can 'ave concerts, like, an' the young lady can play the 'arp!"

But the Head Weasel only shook his head disapprovingly "Stoaty, it ain't civil to go a-teasing 'em, is it? They're 'elpless prisoners, an' you shouldn't go making things still 'arder for them." And to the Rabbit, apologetically, "Never you pay him mind, miss; 'e's low, that's what '*e* is."

"Low, is it?" The Stoat hunched one shoulder and said sullenly, "I was just 'aving a bit of fun. Well, all right then. Knock yerself out, but"—and he rounded upon them fiercely—"*don't* think it'll get you out, you two. These walls are solid as solid, they are." He tapped the back wall, which gave a *thunk* calculated to support his statement.

"Indeed, we're very sorry for bothering you!" said the Rabbit faintly. She found the Stoat's near presence a trifle overpowering. The Toad said nothing at all, for he had fallen to the ground with a little plashing noise, in a dead faint.

The tack-room door slammed behind them, and the lock clicked again. "An' keep it *down!*" the Stoat shouted through the door.

They were more circumspect after that, but (once the Rabbit had roused the Toad, patting his hands and waving the little bottle of *sal volatile* from her reticule beneath his nose) in the end they were able to clear everything away from the corner, aided by the even hiss of the rain, which had settled into a steady rhythm and seemed ready to make a night of it.

There *was* a gap between the floor and the wall, where the bottom of the plank was decayed: too small for anyone larger than a mouse, but the rotten wood came away in spongy bits when the Rabbit pulled at it. Picking at it with her paws and using the strap-cutter she had retrieved from the shelf, she was able to remove still more, until she blunted the tool on the undecayed wood that could not be cut. Lying full-length upon the floor, she carefully stuck her head through the hole, avoiding the ragged edges. Rain dripped from the eaves onto her ears as she looked about. The grassy yard beside the barn was empty of anything but grass and cowpats (even the robin was gone); but beyond it— O happiness! There was the beechwood: separated grey trunks sheathed in silver-green leaves, with any number of clumping shrubs between them. If they could *get* there without being noted, they would be concealed, and the endless sound of the shivering beech leaves and the fresh rain might—*might*—protect them from pursuit, long enough for them to get well out of reach, and then, to the Hills at last!

As for the hole, it was small but she thought she might just be able to get out of it, if she did not mind scraping off the buttons on her bodice or getting her skirt even dirtier, though already she could not contemplate her gown—once her nicest Town-going outfit—without sorrow. Both would be a pity, but she had already lost one of her buttons and sacrifices would be necessary if they were to escape.

"So perhaps after dark," she whispered to the Toad with some satisfaction as she knelt back from the hole and brushed the bits of wood and straw from her skirt. The Toad had been assigned to watch the tack-room door, thus ensuring that the Stoat and Head Weasel did not enter unexpectedly and find the Rabbit at her work, a task which had not taxed him inordinately, for they seemed to have fallen asleep with their backs against the barn's exterior door. She continued, "The Fox said they were all to return tonight, and there will be a lot of noise, I'm sure, and they'll all be drinking that horrid stuff again, I shouldn't wonder—"

"A primitive beverage, but with a certain *louche* charm," said the Toad judiciously. He leaned forward to peek into the corner she had just vacated.

"—but we must take care to learn whether they set guards outside the barn. It will be a dark night with all this rain, so I am sure we may avoid them, and—"

The Toad interrupted her, pointing. "*That* is the hole, Rabbit?"

The Rabbit nodded happily.

"That—*nick*? That *peephole*?"

The Rabbit nodded, a bit less happily.

"Rabbit," he said plaintively, "how am *I* to get through that crevice?"

She looked down at the hole and across at the Toad. "Well, it will be tight," she allowed finally.

"It will be *impossible*," the Toad whispered sadly, and looked down at the impressive expanse of his own waistcoat, stained and torn now. He had a fine figure (for a Toad), distinguished even, as one might say: a little heavyset, yes; round, certainly; in places the critically minded might call it nearly spherical. An admirable figure, a noble figure; but, alas! There was simply too much of it for the hole in the wall. A Rabbit, slim and in the first flush of winsome youth, might squirm her way to freedom through such a chink; a Toad in the full-bodied bloom of the prosperous midafternoon of Life could not.

She took his point immediately, and sat down on the tack truck, a little deflated. "How unfortunate. We shall have to think of something else, then."

But—the—Toad! What came next from him might have been anything: vocal rage against the bitter realities of a life that did not supply larger holes when needed; abject remorse for his laxness with regard to the strict regimen of diet and exercise an eminent London practitioner had ordered some months earlier; gusty weeping; loud lamentations; speechless despair; or some combination of these—for the Toad could shuttle between emotional states, even oppositional ones, as quickly as a leaf can flutter. But no. This time at least, the Toad looked inside and found a better, deeper Toad. He looked down at the hole and said, with a quiet dignity, "Rabbit, *you* must go."

The Rabbit gaped at him. She was an accommodating creature and generally took those around her at whatever value they set for themselves, but *this*—this selflessness, this nobility—was something quite out of the common way for the Toad. "Escape *without* you, you mean?"

"Yes," said the Toad somberly, like Napoleon at Elba. "Go without me. I shall stay until these villains have received their ransom; and if I am not ransomed—well, I hope I know how a gentleman should face adversity."

The Rabbit took one of his paws in hers. "Toad, are you quite well? You don't sound at all like yourself."

He pulled his paw free with a gesture filled with gentle self-abnegation. "And, dear Rabbit—my dear, *dear* Rabbit—if they punish me for your escape, I shall suffer with a smile upon my face, knowing that you at least are free."

The Toad had fixed his eyes upon a point in the middle distance, presenting his left profile, which the Rabbit eyed, concerned, before patting his paw briskly and saying, "Well, I *shan't* go without you, Toad, so this is just talk. We'll find another way, that's all."

He turned his face to her, astonished. "Won't—go!"

She sat back and looked around. "So . . . if there is no way out the back wall, perhaps we might go through the ceiling, after all?"

But the Toad only repeated, "Won't—go!"

"Could we fashion a rope ladder from all the reins and straps? If only I had not dulled the strap-cutter! If we—"

"Won't *go?*" said the Toad, in an altogether different voice. "Spurn my sacrifice? Of course you'll go!"

The subsequent brangle was low-pitched and undertaken in tones that were anything but lofty. Having claimed a moral high ground for himself, the Toad was reluctant to abandon it for any cause whatsoever; but it had to be admitted that the longer he fought with the Rabbit about her refusal to leave him behind, the less he liked the notion of what would happen if she *did* go. And, now that he thought about it (though he admitted he had not always attended in school as he ought to have), had not Napoleon *died* on Elba? Or was it Elba? Toad was vague on the details, but in any case, wherever he had breathed his last, he imagined it was not in the ripe fullness of a happy old age, surrounded by admiring friends and followers.

In the end, he ceded his ground with a certain private (he hoped) relief, and an agreement was made: they would face their situation together for now, but if there seemed to be no other possibility, she would slip out and get help in the Hills—though she wasn't sure what exactly her siblings and their neighbors, the Hedgehogs and the Hares and such, could do against desperate criminals. While she longed to be able to enlist Beryl—to say nothing of the bold Badger, the clever Water Rat, and the staunch Mole—she could never get all the way to the River Bank and back soon enough, not even if she started this very minute.

As night fell, the Weasels and Stoats (and the Barn Rat) returned in twos and threes, greeting the Stoat and Head

Weasel, who had guarded the prisoners, with half-stifled cheers and laughter, as though they had been refreshing themselves from square dark bottles all day. There was much slapping of backs and "'Allo, chums!"-ing, and a great scraping of stool legs and shifting of hay bales upon the barn's main floor, but at last everyone had everything to their liking. The Rabbit had taken advantage of the noise to pick quietly at one of the boards between the tack room and the main floor until she had created a widened crack to press her eye against. She peeped out.

The ruffians had gathered into an irregular circle, loose enough that everyone had a bit of something to prop his back against, but close enough for convenience, for they commenced to pass around a bottle, this one dark green in hue and oval in cross-section. Conversation was general, everyone talking at once and across the circle in the lowest way, which made it hard to pick out any individual speech, but they all seemed cheerful to jollification. Many of them seemed to be planning how they would spend their share of the ransom money.

The list was varied, unified only in that no one quite knew what sums larger than ten pounds might realistically purchase. Some wanted to buy a pub ("I'll call it *The Toad's Despair*," said a Weasel, to a great round of coarse laughter), and others wanted to emigrate to America; if a Stoat spoke enthusiastically of opening a tuck-shop, a Weasel talked longingly of Race Week at Epsom Downs. The Barn Rat discussed the merits of launching his daughter on the *ton*—she was a lovely, elegant lass, if 'e said so 'imself, the very spit of her mother; and that dainty, that she ate 'er chicken with a knife and fork, just like gentry an' all. Gold rings set with cabochon rubies for their paws; platinum watch fobs with watches to which they might be attached; bespoke clothing; visits to the seaside; even motor-cars—and indeed, two Weasels nearly came to blows over the comparative merits of the Gottleib Dasher and the Coventry Guerdon.

"Motor-cars!" said the Toad to the Rabbit (for he also had been listening), "These villains would buy motor-cars at *my* expense! I'll show *them* motor-cars!" And he would have gone on in this vein for some time, save that the Rabbit showed no signs of hearing him at all.

Suddenly the barn door slid open and shouts went up: "The Boss!—'Ey, Chief!—Three cheers for the Boss!—'Ip, 'ip, 'ooray!"

"Quiet, all of you!" snapped the Fox as he entered and closed the door. "I could hear you from half a mile away, boys. We're not rich yet—and we're not safe yet, not by a long chalk."

There was some abashed shuffling of feet. "Sorry, Boss," each outlaw said in turn.

"So what's the plan now, Chief?" asked a Stoat.

"The letters were sent off," replied the Fox. "Fifty thousand pounds for the Toad." An awed murmur ran around the circle. "They'll have no choice, for I didn't give them any way to contact us, just the address for the exchange: a tree behind St Giles's, in the Hills."

The Head Weasel said, "And the young miss?"

The Fox shrugged. "Her too. I set her price at a hundred pounds."

The Rabbit pinned her ears back at this. No one likes to hear herself held cheap, whatever the circumstances.

"I mean after," said the Head Weasel.

"*She* will be freed, of course." There was just enough emphasis on the *she* to set the Rabbit to frowning and the Toad to tugging at her sleeve saying anxiously, "'*She*'? What does he mean—'*she*'?"

The Barn Rat said, "So *when* are they bringing the ransom, Chief?"

"When? I said— Hmm. I said . . ." The Fox trailed off a moment, frowning.

Behind the Rabbit, the Toad was still bleating, "'*She*'? Why not *they*? Did they mean *they*, but only said *she*? Why did they not say *they*?"

"Do you know," said the Fox at last. "I, ah, didn't give them a specific time. It slipped my mind." Consternation; uproar. "Look," said the Fox loudly. "I forgot, that's all! A chap can't think of everything. It won't matter, anyway," he added in a more normal tone of voice as the sound ebbed. "We'll go to the Hills tomorrow and stay until they show up, that's all."

"An' what about the prisoners?" said a Weasel.

"They'll stay here," announced the Fox. "When we double-cross Toad's friends, we don't want them close enough to be rescued, do we, chaps?" Loud laughter. "We'll be hearing from Scotland Yard in the next day, I expect. So we take the ransom money, and then we let *her* go, and turn *him* over to the authorities. And they'll put him back in gaol, and we'll get our pardons, boys!"

The Rabbit gasped. The Toad stumbled back from the wall, repeating through numb lips, "'Double-cross—Scotland Yard—turn him over—back in gaol'! It's over, all over—doomed! Doomed!" And he let out a shivering screech so rich in mingled terror and despair that the brigands all fell silent and stared at the tack-room door with wide, haunted eyes.

"What was *that*?" exclaimed the Fox. He was used to blood-curdling cries in the call of duty, as it were, but this was quite out of the common way.

But the Head Weasel said dismissively, "O, that's the Toad, right enough. 'E's been goin' off like that every so often all day—a-wailing and screeching and cryin' out, 'Doomed!

Doomed!' The Rabbit's ever so much better mannered. A right lady, *she* is."

The Stoat who had spent the day with him on guard added, "If you ignore 'im, 'e settles down to weeping loud, but you get used to that after a while. An' 'e does shut up from time to time, too."

The Fox shuddered. "The sooner he is out of our hands, the better."

The brigands went back to their planning—who was to stay with the prisoners at the barn and who to travel to the churchyard; the negotiations with Scotland Yard; how they would extract the money from the Toad's friends at the churchyard without revealing that the Toad was not present for the exchange—but the Rabbit could no longer attend carefully. She had her paws full with the Toad, now clutching at her ankles while his eyes started nearly from his head as he shrieked, "Doomed!"

There was a noise by the tack room's back wall, as though a tree limb were knocking against it, and then there was a voice.

It was the Mole.

Chapter Eleven
Escape

The Mole and Beryl made excellent time on their journey. As children, they had spent their days rambling together through the Hills near their home: long, satisfying tramps in any weather with no goal but the pleasure of the long rolling downs under their paws. If the situation had not been so dire, this walk through the country would have filled each of them with that same quiet pleasure: everything ripe or ripening so that the air was filled with the heady smells of fruit and grain, the heavy scent of late-summer roses (so much graver than roses in springtime), the slight sweetness of the pollen that floated everywhere and gave the air a golden cast that made the world seem gilt. Their travel was harmonious, with only the minimal squabbling all siblings seem unable to resist, even siblings who generally like one another and are currently engaged upon some shared, important task: a few small disagreements about which fork of a road to follow, a bit of grousing about how early in the morning one should get started; but the number of times that Beryl said, "Well, *really*, Mole!" and the Mole said, "Do stop *bossing*, Beryl!" were very few.

One such moment came at about in the evening of the first day, when Beryl paused to speak with two Squirrels who were standing in the path, gossiping. The Mole watched impatiently just out of earshot, shifting his weight from paw to paw and muttering, "Come *on!*"; but when she at last came over to him it seemed to have been worth it, for she had news: there were doings involving Stoats, Weasels, and such folks at an abandoned barn a few miles from where they were, and not so very far from St Giles's church in the Hills.

"And that," Beryl concluded, "must be where Toad and the Rabbit are."

"Are you sure?" said the Mole.

She looked at him quizzically. "It stands to reason, surely? We know they are kidnapped, and their captors will wish to keep them somewhere close to what I believe is called the exchange point, yet not too close. It would be a great coincidence if there were *two* gangs of hoodlums conniving in so limited an area. At any rate, my editor should never permit me to get away with it if I were to include something like this in one of my novels."

"But life is not like novels!" said the Mole.

"It is like novels more often than anyone would like to admit," said Beryl with a certain regret, "only not so interesting."

The Mole said unhappily, "I suppose you're right. But it is hard, that there should be an entire *gang* of kidnappers and not merely one or two individuals. What are we going to do?"

"Collect more information," said Beryl, who had not written *The Iron Hare of Chateau Sang* for nothing. "Let's go to the barn and find out what's what. If we can, we'll free Toad and the Rabbit; and if we can't, then we'll keep an eye on them until they're moved to the church, and the Water Rat and the Badger arrive with the money for the ransom. It would be too bad that a band of criminals will get so much of Toad's wealth, but it's better than the alternative."

"O, I agree," said the Mole fervently. "Off we go, then."

And off they did go, though their tempers ran a little short the next day, after the rain began and didn't seem as though it would ever stop. Soaked to the skin, they trudged forward, following narrow roads and hollow lanes, and hiding whenever they heard the sounds of anyone approaching. At times (but, fortunately for the fates of the Toad and the Rabbit, at different times), it seemed to each of them that this was a fool's errand unlikely to end in success, and that it would make more sense to go straight to whichever village was closest, hand the whole thing over to the local constabulary, and let the Toad take his chances in court. Then, too, the gossiping Squirrels had not been quite as precise as they needed to be for Beryl and the Mole to find the barn without trouble, and so there was further delay while Mole chatted with a suspicious-seeming Lizard, trying to get better directions without showing their intentions too clearly.

But in the end, they found the barn. They crept up through the beechwood, and from the shelter of a dogwood bush at the bottom of the little grassy field they watched the bandits trickle in as evening fell: some Weasels, some Stoats, a Barn Rat, and finally (here the Mole tapped Beryl on the arm and they exchanged concerned glances) a Fox. The Fox—clearly the leader, but they would have expected nothing less from a Fox—set a guard at the barn door, a single Weasel who settled down immediately and pulled out some grimy dice, which he tossed from paw to paw. The door was pulled shut.

Beryl and the Mole slipped unobserved to the barn walls, and heard voices: rough, low voices (though they couldn't hear quite what was being said) and quite a lot of coarse laughter. It seemed to be a meeting of some sort. "But how shall we find out if Toad and the Rabbit are here?" breathed the Mole into Beryl's ear. "They could be anywhere!"

But most conveniently for them, they heard it: a voice that was not that of a Stoat or a Weasel: a wretched voice, the quavering voice of one of the more severely Damned, a lost soul wailing as though he were being boiled by devils on a particularly ill-tempered day. It was the Toad, right enough, and after that, it was the matter of a moment for the rescuers to circle the barn until they came to the correct section of the wall.

"Toad?" whispered the Mole into a crack. *"Toad?"*

There was a pause, then: "Mole?" came the Rabbit's voice through a chink in the wall.

"Rabbit!" exclaimed the Mole, stating the obvious. He grinned at Beryl.

She leaned forward. "I'm here too, Rabbit! We've come to rescue you!"

"O, I do hope you can!" whispered the Rabbit. "You have no idea how dull this is—not that Toad isn't *perfectly* congenial company—" There was an awkward momentary pause, for no one could believe her (Toad was still howling "Doomed!" periodically, and had not yet noticed what was happening at the back of the tack room), and even the Rabbit, that most light-hearted of souls, sounded guilty at so patent a lie. "We have been trapped here for *days*, and I have not been able to make a hole big enough to get us out."

The Mole said, "A hole, you say?"

The Toad had been having a very hard time of it these past two days. He had slept upon a blanket that smelt of horses and mildew. He had eaten dry bread of a depressingly brown hue, without roast beef, cheese, mustard, gherkins, or any of the other civilizing forces that might have improved it. He had drunk water from a pail without ice or even a splash of something to make it go down more easily. He had been denied a toothbrush, a clothespress, a valet, and a hot bath. He had behaved very well despite the near hopelessness of his situation; and so, now that he had given in to despair—*real* despair, he knew, not some pale on-again, off-again imitation—he felt as though he rather deserved the chance to do the thing thoroughly.

He was so wrapped up in his wailing that he had heard none of the whispering, and so one may imagine his surprise when out of the dark corner behind the feedbox popped Beryl, exactly as though she had been conjured in a pantomime. "Why, Beryl!" he exclaimed loudly. She was across the little room in a step and threw her paw over his mouth, but there was a sudden ominous silence from the main area.

"Shh!" she hissed in his ear. "Don't let them know!"

For nearly the first time in his life, the Toad acted with presence of mind in an emergency, and so cleverly that he liked to think of it in later years, just before falling asleep. After scarcely a moment, he cried loudly, "Peril! O, peril! Doom!" He trailed off a minute later, when he was further flabbergasted by the Mole appearing just as Beryl had, panting a little and minus some of his buttons (he was somewhat stouter than Beryl); but the day had been saved: the Stoats and Weasels were back at their discussions again.

The Rabbit quickly brought them up to date on the situation. "So what are we to do?" she ended. "There are nine of them—and one is a Fox, and you know how *they* are—and there are only four of us. And we cannot simply slip out the way you came; or rather, I might, but it is not possible for Toad, alas."

They all looked at the Toad, who drew himself up, looking wretched and shamefaced. "I know—I know! It's *my* fault we can't just escape. I've tried slimming programs— I've tried exercise regimens— I've tried salt water and electricity— I've tried Mesmerism— Useless, all useless." He choked back a sob.

Beryl mused, "Rabbit, you said some of the criminals are leaving for St Giles tomorrow, yes?" The Rabbit nodded. "Then we shall just have to wait until there are fewer here, and break you out then."

"But how?" whispered the Mole. "There will still be four or five of them, and there'll only be the two of us until we can get the door to this room unlocked."

"Perhaps we might start from inside?" said Beryl. "Tomorrow, after they are fewer, we could slip back into this room, and then get them to open the door somehow and rush them!"

The Mole frowned. "That's no good. We left a letter for the Badger and the Water Rat. They'll be bringing the ransom to the churchyard. If we wait, we shan't be able to stop them from handing over the ransom."

The Toad, who had been staring at his paws despairingly, started up with horror on his face and gargled out a single word. "No!"

"We may have to accept that as an unfortunate necessity, Toad," said Beryl sternly. "We simply *cannot* fight them all, that's all there is to it."

"There's more, Beryl!" said the Rabbit. "They mean not to free the Toad in *any* case! After they take the ransom, they are going to turn him in to Scotland Yard, in exchange for pardons for their gang."

The Toad choked out another sob.

"*That's* a lot of cheek from them!" said Beryl. "Take poor Toad's money and then send him to gaol anyway? *Really!*" There was a moment's silence, broken only by the Toad's weeping, as they dwelt on the perfidy of bandits.

"But we don't have any weapons, in any case," the Rabbit said sadly. "I've searched and searched, but nothing in here is useful at all, unless we wish to throw horseshoes at them. They took away my pocketknife, even."

"You may have *my* pocketknife," said Beryl, who as an Authoress never travelled without one. "But I do think throwing horseshoes is a *famous* idea, Lottie."

The Mole was understandably a little smug when he said, "But we're not *completely* unarmed. I brought a few things." He pulled from his waistcoat the pistol he had taken from Rat's house, and slapped his paw upon his cutlass, which he had been wearing tucked into his belt—for it was not merely stoutness that had made passage through the hole in the wall difficult for the Mole.

And then Beryl pulled from a hidden pocket of her skirt a dainty but very serviceable pistol with a pearl handle and a silver barrel—and a leather-covered blackjack, small but ruthlessly efficient-looking.

"Beryl!" exclaimed the Mole, forgetting to be quiet. "You—thug!"

"Shh," hissed Beryl, the Rabbit, and the Toad together. They listened for a second (even the Toad, who was becoming interested in the plans for his rescue in spite of himself), but it seemed all right: they could still hear a Weasel and the Fox speaking, and others chiming in, "'Ear, 'ear!"

"Beryl!" the Mole said more softly. "A pistol? A *truncheon?*"

She blushed faintly but only said, "One must be sensible, Mole! So, this is our plan, then: Mole and I shall leave. We'll find boughs in the beechwood that may be used as cudgels, and we'll bring them with us when we return tomorrow, after some of the gang are gone to St Giles's. We shall sneak back into this room through the hole—Toad or Rabbit shall trick the remaining bandits into opening this door—and then we shall all attack at once, and subdue them!"

"And whack 'em and whack 'em and whack 'em," murmured the Toad with a wide, absent smile on his face, as though he were in a delightful trance.

The Mole paused; he had been on the verge of handing the cutlass to the Toad, but it occurred to him that to do so at this moment might encourage the sort of noisy, dramatic outbreak on Toad's part that might bring down the entire gang upon them and ruin all their plans. Instead, he said only, "And if they don't open the door tomorrow, we're not worse off than we are now. Beryl and I will just slip out and think of something else."

"Slip out without me? Leaving me *behind?*" said the Toad, coming down from his Parnassian heights.

The Mole said, "Toad, only for a moment! We would just sneak out and come back through the main barn door, and rescue you that way!"

"No, no," said the Toad. "There's no need. Save yourselves. It's the only sensible thing to do, I know that. It's just— Moley, Scotland Yard! Prison!" His voice was getting a little loud again. "Just—leave me the cutlass. They shan't take me alive!"

"Toad, shut *up,*" hissed the Mole, Beryl, and the Rabbit. But it was too late. The tack room door burst open. For one instant, exactly as though they had all been woven into a tapestry of a genre found in the Great Halls of the better sort of medieval castle, the two forces faced one another: on the one hand, the Heroes—the Mole, armed with pistol and cutlass; Beryl, with a shining pistol in one paw and her blackjack in the other (though, in light of the pistols, a better comparison might be the pen-and-ink illustration for a serial adventure in a Saturday magazine); the Toad, paws curled into unconscious fists; and the Rabbit behind them, looking fierce yet feminine—and against them, casting towering shadows from the dark lantern: the Fox, the Barn Rat, and a veritable horde of Stoats and Weasels.

Here is where Quality will tell. The Mole and (we must not forget, though it is quite easy to do so) the Toad were seasoned veterans of battle. Had they not driven entire armies of Stoats and Weasels from Toad Hall only the year before? There had been only four champions that time, as well—the Mole, the Toad, the Water Rat and the Badger—and while it is true that on that occasion they had been armed to the teeth and their foes had not expected the assault, still a Mole enraged is a force to be reckoned with in any circumstance, and the unpredictability of a beleaguered Toad ought not but strike trepidity into even the most hardened of foes.

The heroes wasted not a moment. The Mole tossed the cutlass to the Toad and charged forward, giving his awful war cry, "A Mole! A Mole!" Beryl ran beside him, silent and with her pistol raised. The Toad, entangled for a moment with the cutlass but straightening himself out quickly, ripped his weapon from its scabbard and leapt forward just behind them, bellowing, "A Toad! A Toad!" which had not the benefit of being original but was at least loud and unsettling. The Rabbit was in the rear, with her paws full of horseshoes.

All might not have gone so well for the River Bank champions, save that a lucky first shot from the Mole's pistol severed a rope and dropped a feed bucket upon the Fox's head, rendering him temporarily *hors de combat*. Beryl fired and a Stoat threw himself backward howling, "I'm 'it! I'm 'it!" before scrambling away—patently not true, she knew, for she had aimed some feet over his head and was accounted a very fair shot, having learnt to fire pistols in her researches for *M. Bourne, Vivisectionist*. The massed enemy fell back a few paces and, as she and the Mole shot again, farther still. The Heroes surged forward.

But alas! Virtue seldom wins the day easily. The grim struggle against Villainy is ever long. The fight was a desperate one: the Heroes striving to reach the barn door, and the bandits pressing them back, all by the light of a single dark lantern which cast crazed, flying shadows as the Stoats and Weasels dodged and wove around the outnumbered River Bankers. Beryl and the Mole shot until their pistols were empty, but their unwillingness to injure anyone, though commendatory to their character, operated against them practically. Soon they found their bullets exhausted and fell back on less sophisticated weapons: Beryl's blackjack and an ancient cricket bat that Mole found leaning against a wall.

The enemies were initially reluctant to engage with the ladies, shoving them aside to get at the Toad and the Mole, or even sidestepping them altogether; but Beryl's efficiency with the blackjack won the heartfelt if pained admiration of many, while the Rabbit, who had been ladies' quoits champion in her parish before she left the Hills and could cover the hob any time she liked, clipped foe after foe with her horseshoes, forcing them to stagger from the fray spouting blood as they clutched their ears, foreheads, or noses. In fact, the ladies were sufficiently dangerous that everyone overcame their reluctance to hit females, and the fighting grew hotter.

How to record a battle so fierce, so desperate! Impossible to show it all; the pen fails and imperfect words hang limp upon the air. A vile Stoat dashes in from the side with a knife in one paw—swings—and jumps back before the Toad can reply as such a dastardly stroke deserves. A base Weasel leaps at the Rabbit, grasping for her arm—she pulls away and swings wildly with the horseshoe in her paw; it connects—he is fallen! An underhanded Barn Rat stretches out a long leg to trip the Mole—he stumbles and nearly falls, wrests himself upright, and swings a doughty reply. Another Stoat (and there are many) slashes with his sword at Beryl—she twists aside, steps in—and coshes him!

And yet, the battle was not an even one. The heroes made it to the barn's door and slipped through, but the bandits surged after them, and now all heard the Fox's voice, conscious again and crying out, "Get 'em, lads!" in a tone that did not bode well, should they be got. They ran across the grassy yard toward the dark beechwood: Beryl first, then the Mole and the Rabbit, and the Toad laboring behind; but it was not going to be enough: the bandits were too close and too many.

The Toad tripped upon a rock and fell flat, losing his cutlass. "Toady!" cried the Mole, and ran back to drag him to his feet; then together they, too, ran into the beechwood behind the others.

"Can't—breathe—" puffed the Toad, but the Mole bodily dragged him on.

They piled into Beryl, who had stopped suddenly, Rabbit nearly losing her balance as she narrowly avoided overrunning them all.

"In front of us!" Beryl cried, and they could all hear it now: crackling, rustling noises in the woods ahead of them, the sounds of animals approaching at a run. They set themselves back to back and waited.

"Doomed!" screamed the Toad.

Chapter Twelve
Return to the River Bank

As it happened, it was the Water Rat and the Badger.
If the Mole and Beryl had travelled quickly,
the Water Rat and the Badger had *raced*. It was
easy to follow the Moles' trail: "Such a nice
couple, asking for the church," an old Mouse-
wife had said with an indulgent smile; "an' I'm sure I wish
them the best, I do!" The Water Rat and the Badger had
exchanged glances and pressed on. When they heard
that the "charming couple" (which elicited more glances)
had changed their direction and were instead, for reasons
unknown, heading for an old barn that had of late become
a haunt for bandits, they did not stop to ask themselves *why*
and *wherefore*, but had rushed on. They were coming along
the hollow lane when they heard shouts and the clash of
arms, and then, astonishing to them both, the Toad's clear
voice crying, "Take—that! And—that!" They ran into the
beechwoods, and found their friends.

It was, as the Rabbit might perhaps put it, all very exciting.
The Badger swung his great stick, tossing Weasels to one side
and Stoats to the other while the Water Rat loosed his pistol
over the heads of the enemy and then waded in with a cudgel
in one paw and the pistol reversed in the other, intent upon
subjugating the Barn Rat; bloody was the battle, but in the

end, the Water Rat conquered, and the Barn Rat collapsed in a heap before him.

The addition to the River Bankers' ranks of what seemed to the Stoats and Weasels to be a dozen Badgers the size of cart horses, and a score of Water Rats who shot fire from their glowing red eyes, deflated any ambitions they might have had. They scattered, but the Mole and Beryl also seemed to be everywhere, clouting them until they cringed upon the ground, clutching their heads and injured limbs, and begging for mercy. As for the Fox? Sneaky as all his kind are, as soon as he saw the way the wind was blowing, he tried to slip away into the beechwood but was unhappily (for him) perceived doing so by the Badger, who followed on swift paws and struck him down.

It was the work of only a few minutes for Beryl and the Water Rat to tie them all up with bits of the rope from Beryl's pack: the Rat was of course familiar with anything at all that had to do with boats, knots included; and as for Beryl, an Authoress is mistress of many skills, and Beryl's researches for *The Haunted Treasure of Bone Island* had included knots. Even now she could weave a Monkey's Fist or a Turk's Head (her knotwork bell-pulls were a popular holiday gift in the family); efficiently tying up criminals was child's play to her.

"Now, what should we do with these ruffians?" said the Water Rat, leaning heavily on his cutlass, and panting, for he was still out of breath.

"Whack 'em, and whack 'em, and whack 'em!" cried the Toad in ecstasy.

"No, I have a better idea," said Beryl. "They were going to turn Toad in to Scotland Yard and receive a pardon. Why not turn the tables upon them?"

The Mole gave a cheer. "Hurrah, Beryl, that's really very clever! Let's do it!"

Beryl blushed and said, "O, pooh, you would have thought of it yourself, if I had not."

The Badger looked from Beryl to the Mole; clearly an understanding flourished between them. When he glanced across to the Water Rat, he saw that he, too, had noted this, and was looking a little unhappy. But he had no wish to be churlish, and was steeling himself to accept a difficult truth, so he said only, "Beryl, as always, a very sensible notion. We will find out from this scoundrel"—he nudged the Fox with one paw—"how he was meaning to contact the authorities, and then we will turn them in, and receive a pardon for the Toad. Yes," he said, more happily, "that *will* work very well."

And so they dragged the Stoats and Weasels and the Barn Rat and the Fox back to the barn and piled them in the middle of the main room's floor, where they could be kept an eye on while the Badger and Beryl went into the nearest village and arranged for them to be taken away. After a while a closed wagon arrived, into which the criminals were slung without ceremony; a policeman shook Badger's paw and nodded politely to Beryl; and then they were gone.

The Toad had been hiding in the beechwood but rushed up as soon as the constables were gone. "Am I pardoned? Am I pardoned?" he cried, and began capering about.

"Not yet," said the Badger, but he looked pleased. "These are just the local force, taking custody. But we were right—they've been trying to catch these culprits for some time, and it was very much against the grain to pardon them. I don't think we'll have much trouble getting your pardon, but you will have to be patient."

The Toad leapt with joy. "Free! Ha, ha—yet another bullet dodged! Not even Scotland Yard can keep me—crashed a motor-cycle—a complete pardon! Toad—great as always! He, he!"

"You are not pardoned *yet*," warned Beryl with some desperation. "Toad, you must live quietly until then."

"I'll be the patientest Toad that ever was! You'll see!"

The Badger met Beryl's eyes with an expression that said, "I *told* you how it would be!" but said aloud only, "You're right, Toad—because I am staying with you until it is complete."

"Couldn't be better!" said the Toad genially. "Always happy to have you under my roof—always a welcome guest—for any amount of time, of course. He, he— Free!" It was clear that yet again he was lost to anything of sense that might be said to him; but everyone knew that was just Toad's way, and no one minded much.

The trip home should have felt like a triumphal procession: the Toad and the Rabbit had been saved from their imprisonment with no injuries to the River Bank party, and it seemed likely that the Toad could be saved from Scotland Yard, as well, by means of the pardon the Badger meant to get for him—and all without sacrificing a penny of Toad's £50,000, or even the Rabbit's £100; but in fact, the whole journey had a sour feel.

For one thing, it began raining again, and, while the Mole, Beryl, the Water Rat, and the Badger were all equipped for overland travel, the Toad and the Rabbit had nothing but the ragged Town clothes they stood up in. The rain was neither hard nor cold, but it came down steadily and soon everyone was soaked to the skin. Nothing in anyone's packs could be made to fit Toad, who went off into convulsive fits of shivering whenever he noticed that anyone was looking at him. "I'm— fine," he would gasp out. "Nothing to—worry about! We Toads have—weak chests—indeed, my dear father . . . But I don't mean to complain—we don't *always* die . . . even in situations nearly this bad. A doctor and a hot bath—a mustard plaster—I *might* be spared—perhaps some hot gin-and-lemon—and at least I will die pardoned," and he would go off into such an outburst of coughing that the soft-hearted Mole would say to the others, "Hear that? We *must* get him somewhere away from this weather!" and even the Water Rat would say, "It's just Toad shamming as usual, but it's going to be a miserable long slog if he's going to gas like this all the way back."

In the end, matters came to a head when the Toad simply collapsed; and it mattered less that he might be faking it than that, faking or not, they couldn't carry him all the way to the River Bank upon their backs, not with the best will in the world. But here they ran into their second problem: paying for rooms at an inn—if they could find an inn at all: barring that, a friendly farmhouse—was impossible, let alone paying for a doctor and the gin-and-lemon and all the rest. The Mole and Beryl had not come out with more than a few coins, for they had been in a hurry when they left. The Toad had nothing at all because of having thrown it away in Town. Even though she had spent nearly everything, the Rabbit had more money than any of them; but pin money for a Rabbit was in no way sufficient for the needs of a Toad accustomed to traveling in the first style of luxury, a Toad, further, who was going to need nursing and who *knew* what else.

"But it'll be fine!" said the Mole cheerily. "Ratty and Badger brought Toad's ransom, didn't they? We'll just use a bit of that—"

The Toad sat up suddenly, his coughing momentarily silenced.

"Ransom?" said the Badger and the Water Rat together.

"Why, the fifty thousand pounds the Fox and his gang were demanding for the Toad's safe return," said the Mole. "It was all in the ransom note I left for you. You—you didn't receive that?" he faltered, looking at their faces.

"We did not," said the Badger, looking dark.

The Water Rat added, "You mentioned a letter, but we looked everywhere and it wasn't there. Moley, are you sure you enclosed it?"

"Positive," said the Mole, absently patting his pockets, as one does when something small is mislaid.

"Well," said the Mole a few minutes later, after the ransom note was discovered and confessed to, and the Water Rat had expressed himself somewhat freely about chaps losing their heads if they were not sewn on; and the Mole had apologized, looking ashamed and miserable; and the Toad had relaxed (since the money wasn't available to be spent, after all); and the Badger had said, "Now, now: there's no need to go on about it, Rat; it doesn't matter that we didn't know about the ransom since we didn't have to pay it, after all"; and Beryl had suggested that everyone might perhaps take a deep breath and calm down;—after all that, the Mole said, "Well, if you *weren't* coming to pay the ransom—"

The Water Rat made a grinding noise with his teeth.

"—then why *were* you coming?" The Mole looked at them, curiosity plain in his honest face. "We're deeply grateful that you showed up when you did, but it is very odd, you know."

Since the rescue, the Badger's expression had been dour, and all the more so whenever he observed the Mole and Beryl as they helped one another over a stile or exchanged a soft word; and also, whenever he saw the Rabbit offer her paw to the Toad, as he staggered weakly along, saying, "Just a little farther, dear Toad ! You can do it, I know you can!" and the Toad replied feebly, "For you, Rabbit, I shall try!" Now it grew darker still. He harumphed, and glared at a broad stone wall they were approaching.

"Ah," said the Water Rat. "Well. Badger can probably explain it better than I can. He's the chap for explaining things!"

"We came to rescue you," said the Badger.

"From what?" asked Beryl. "Without the ransom note, you had no notion we were going into danger!"

The Water Rat stared at Beryl. "Well, ah . . . That is to say—"

"Sit down," said the Badger gravely. "Beryl, you and Mole, sit there." He pointed to a pile of rocks that had been cleared from the field of beans they had been crossing, and then to the stone wall: "And you, Rabbit, and you, Toad, sit there—for Heaven's sake, Toad, don't sprawl there in the dirt like a house cat—*sit* there."

Everyone sat as instructed. The Water Rat stood off to one side, looking for all the world like an aide-de-camp hearing the orders at Salamanca.

The Badger rubbed a paw over his face. "You all know—well, some of you, anyway: you, Toad; and Mole and Rat—that I am not a proponent of matrimony. It is, in my opinion, the end of all comfort, an unnatural state full of brangling, needless disputations, and social obligations requiring tight collars and absurd demands for quite unnecessary changes of linen. . . ." He fell silent, brooding upon the enormities of wedlock.

They waited patiently for a few moments. Then Beryl said, "Badger, are you well?"

"I am never ill," said the Badger heavily.

"But why all this talk of matrimony? It's relevant to nothing," she said.

He shook his shaggy head. "There's no way to wrap this up cleanly, no way to sweeten the pill. You must be wed."

Their voices tumbled over one other in their surprise and confusion: "We must be . . . *what?*"—"Wed?"—"Who?"—"Are you *sure* you're all right, Badger?"

"*All* of you," replied the Badger. "Not all together, I mean: you, Toad, must wed the Rabbit. And you, Mole, must wed Beryl."

There was a silence.

The Badger went on "Beryl, Rabbit, you have each travelled with a male, unaccompanied by any second female to lend you countenance. I *know*"—he emphasized the word in a minatory way—"that the Mole and the Toad will demonstrate their decency, dignity, and propriety and offer you the shelter of their names."

Beryl began laughing, and the Badger grew prickly. "It is *not* a laughing matter, Miss Mole. You are heedless. You do not realize—"

"Pooh!" said Beryl. "I know, I don't mean to laugh at you at all, and I apologize. But you are exactly like the father in a serialized novel! This is not the way things are any more, Badger. I should only marry if I chose to—which I do not."

And now Mole was laughing a little, as well: "And she cannot marry me, anyway, not if it were ever so. Beryl is my sister."

"Your—sister!" gasped everyone save the Rabbit, who only stared at the rest, surprised; she of course had known since the beginning, and had thought everyone else did, too.

The Water Rat said, "So *that* is why you avoided her so! Your *elder* sister, by chance?" The Mole and Beryl nodded. He continued, "Of *course*. It all makes sense now," and he went off in a peal of laughter that left him snorting and wiping his eyes.

The Toad had been thinking all this while. He was a flighty Toad, a frivolous Toad, a Toad abandoned to every sort of vanity and folly, but he was also at heart a decent Toad, and he could not but admit the justice of the Badger's words. He had been days in the Rabbit's company without any duenna, any chaperone or maid or female companionship at all. No one would have been happier than he to have been able at this moment to reveal that the Rabbit was his sister; but she was not and he could not. He rose from his seat and, after making sure he would not be placing himself uncomfortably upon a stone or twig, lowered himself to one knee before the Rabbit.

"Madam," said the Toad to the Rabbit, "will you do me the honor of accepting my hand in marriage?"

He thought he got it off rather well, with the perfect note of respectful yet ardent admiration, but the Rabbit, regrettably, only giggled.

The Toad, disregarding the giggle and rather getting into the spirit of things, added grandiloquently, "I am sure that your family and friends will wish to judge for themselves my ability to sustain a wife in a manner suitable to her class and character. I should be happy to lay out my situation fully for whomever—"

"She can't marry Toad!" interrupted the Water Rat, and, into the silence that followed his words, he dropped, "He's disgraced. He's still a criminal! At least, until there's a pardon he can't be married, not without involving his, ah, bride in his disgrace." It was a wrench to get the word out, but he succeeded. The Toad visibly brightened.

"The more reason to clear his name quickly," said the Badger, who was starting to think rather well of this notion. It was universally known that marriage cooled the blood in the veins, so perhaps it might settle even the mercurial Toad.

"Disgraced?" said the Rabbit hotly. "You speak as though it were *Toad's* fault that things went wrong, and that is nonsense, as anyone with sense can see. And in any case, it was all very exciting. I'm sure any bride of Toad's would have a delightful time of it." She smiled fondly down upon the Toad, who had clasped her paw between his own.

"My *dear*," said the Toad with appropriate fervor. The Water Rat looked rather ill.

"But," said the Rabbit, "I don't think so." And she pulled her paw free.

"You're *rejecting* me?" said the Toad. "Me? Toad? *The* Toad? Toad of Toad Hall? Myself?"

"I am," said the Rabbit cheerfully. "Let me see if I say this correctly: 'I am deeply sensible of the honor you have shown me, and sorry for any pain my refusal may cause—' Is that quite right, Beryl?"

Beryl nodded. "That is precisely as I had Evelina say it in *19 Croquet Lane*."

They exchanged a smile, then Rabbit turned back to the Toad, and with a tiny curtsey said, "—but I must decline your very kind offer."

"But—!" said the Badger, faint but pursuing. "Your good name!"

The Rabbit gave a little shake. "O, that! No, Toad's a very good sort, but I have no wish to be trammeled with a husband."

"'Trammeled'? 'A very good sort'?" Toad said, puffing up. "*This* is all you feel for me? When I have offered you my hand, Toad Hall, and my heart?"

The Rabbit shook her head. "It is very good of you, indeed it is! But no. No husbands for me!"

The rest of the walk home was silent. The Rabbit's rejection of the Toad's marriage proposal seemed to have cured his incipient cold, at least, and if he drooped along at the tail of the group, counting syllables on his paws, and muttering to himself, "Love, glove, above; lost, tossed, frost . . .," it did no harm to anyone else, and did not slow them up in the slightest.

And so they came again to the River Bank. It was dusk, and the air was filled with the liquid melodies of nightingales and reed warblers, and the stridulence of the frogs and crickets; dusk, when the air thickened and settled as mist on the River; and for the first time there was something else in the air, a snap that was not yet autumn but would be, in a few weeks' time.

The Badger went home with the Toad, avowedly to assist should Toad Hall have been overrun by Stoats in their absence (it was not) but in fact to keep a close eye on the Toad until the pardon was final— "Or a foot upon his neck, if that's what it takes," muttered the Badger to the Water Rat as they separated.

For several weeks, the Toad went nowhere and did nothing. The Badger had explained the importance of behaving well; the Toad had agreed fervently and shed not a few tears at the past follies that had so stained his name and character that the Badger (rightly) felt he could not return to his own home in the Wild Wood but must watch the Toad carefully. The Badger knew better than to take this remorse as writ on anything but sand, and so he stuck like glue to the Toad, an omnipresent rain cloud casting gloom over all his waking hours, until the Badger in desperation proposed the Toad take up a quiet hobby, such as collecting Coins of the Ancient World. To the astonishment of all, the Toad did precisely that, and for some time after, Toad Hall was a flurry of special couriers whirling in from Town, bringing numismatic catalogues and worn, ragged little fragments of silver or gold wrapped in cotton wool. "Toad taken advantage of?" said the Badger to the Mole one day, when they were all gathered for luncheon at Toad Hall. "Of course he's being taken advantage of! But at least it's not motor-cycles."

As for his passion for the Rabbit, so momentarily felt and so sincerely expressed, it did not last the composition of even a full quatrain, let alone an entire sonnet. The Rabbit, instead, remained with her dear friend.

Beryl returned to her cottage and wrote her books. *Philotera's Horror* was followed by *The Dark Overture*, and after that she began a long and ambitious four-book series which she and her publisher hoped would bring the latter days of the Roman Empire to startling life, and which might break her into the American Market, so fiercely coveted by all English authors. She spent her afternoons on the River, or visiting the many friends she had made: the Mouse-wives and Hedgehog misses, and even some of the younger Weasels of both sexes, who found her novels very dashing (to put it mildly), and eyed her with mingled awe and wariness.

She and the Badger became good friends, and even in the winter, when most social life on the River Bank slowed to a crawl, one or the other would occasionally rouse sufficiently to pay a call upon the other.

The Water Rat remained a little suspicious of her, still worried that she might in some fashion disrupt the friendships of the River Bank, but as time passed and he saw that she did nothing of the sort, and indeed had no wish to do so, he warmed to her company and even went so far as to solicit her company on summer afternoons. She was quiet and did not talk too much (unlike, say, the Toad), she made excellent lemonade, and she was well content to let the Water Rat do the rowing. By midwinter, it became an understood thing that on certain sunny days he would walk across to Sunflower Cottage, for she loaned her books freely without asking for a speedy return and could be coaxed into talking about writing, a thing the Water Rat at least never tired of.

Beryl and the Mole settled into a new relationship, as well: grown up but with all the history of shared childhood. They did not often visit one another's homes, but would go on long rambles together, even as far as the Hills to visit their siblings, and such was their harmony that one might spend a day in their company and see no more than a few instances of eye-rolling, or hear more than a barest minimum of heavy sighs.

Author's Note

In 1908, Methuen Books published a novel that became one of the classics of children's literature, *The Wind in the Willows*. Its author, Kenneth Grahame, was a writer of sentimental memoirs and novels in what were turning out to be the dying days of the British Empire.

As a child, I adored this book, and the animals that peopled the River Bank—staunch Mole, the sociable Water Rat, the severe Badger, and the ebullient, ever troublesome Toad. I didn't notice the entrenched assumptions about privilege, class, and gender. Later, as an adult, these things bothered me; this book is an imperfect attempt to open up the world of the River Bank a little.

I wish to acknowledge Diane Purkiss and G. S. Dastur, who offered many, many suggestions that contributed to the book's tone and details. Thank you also to readers Will Badger, Wilton Barnhardt, Leigh Dragoon, and Lane Robins, but a special thank-you to Elizabeth Bourne and Barbara Webb. Much love.

About the Author
& Illustrator

Kij Johnson has won the Hugo, Nebula, World Fantasy, and Sturgeon Awards for her short fiction. She is also the author of four novels, a print novella, and a collection, *At the Mouth of the River of Bees: Stories*. She teaches writing at the University of Kansas, where she is associate director for the Gunn Center for the Study of Science Fiction. She splits her time between Kansas and Washington.

Kathleen Jennings was raised on fairytales in western Queensland. She trained as a lawyer and filled the margins of her notes with pen and ink illustrations. She has been nominated for the World Fantasy award and has received several Ditmar Awards. She lives in Brisbane, Australia.